W0006205

SECOND TIME
LOVE

SEAL Brotherhood: Legacy Series
Book 9

SHARON HAMILTON

ABOUT THE BOOK

On the eve of his stepdaughter's wedding, Navy SEAL Trace Bennett receives an urgent cry for help from an unexpected source—the bride's father, Tony, his wife's ex-husband who is about to be released from prison.

As the celebration ends, Trace rushes to Portland to aid Tony, a former NBA star who has fallen from grace.

Weeks later, while Gretchen and the girls remain in San Diego, Trace deploys with SEAL Team 3 to the Canary Islands and North Africa. From across the globe, Trace's contacts uncover a sinister group known as "The Organization," which operates a dark network involved in gambling, child prostitution, and human trafficking. This group targets Tony to settle old gambling debts, but now they also threaten to harm Trace's family while he's overseas.

As the situation intensifies, Trace must find a way to safeguard his loved ones and take down this vile organization, all without compromising his principles or his SEAL integrity. Racing against time, he battles to protect his family and eradicate the evil that preys on those he cherishes.

This captivating novel is a tale of second-time love, even sweeter than before. It continues the gripping saga from "SEAL My Love," Book 9 of the original SEAL Brotherhood Series, which narrates the heart-warming journey of how Trace and Gretchen found each other, leading to him becoming the loving father and husband that they truly deserved.

SHARON HAMILTON'S BOOK LIST

SEAL BROTHERHOOD BOOKS

SEAL BROTHERHOOD SERIES
Accidental SEAL Book 1

Fallen SEAL Legacy Book 2

SEAL Under Covers Book 3

SEAL The Deal Book 4

Cruisin' For A SEAL Book 5

SEAL My Destiny Book 6

SEAL of My Heart Book 7

Fredo's Dream Book 8

SEAL My Love Book 9

SEAL Encounter Prequel to Book 1

SEAL Endeavor Prequel to Book 2

Ultimate SEAL Collection Vol. 1 Books 1-4 /
2 Prequels

Ultimate SEAL Collection Vol. 2 Books 5-9

SEAL BROTHERHOOD LEGACY SERIES
Watery Grave Book 1

Honor The Fallen Book 2

Grave Injustice Book 3

Deal With The Devil Book 4

Cruisin' For Love Book 5

Destiny of Love Book 6

Heart of Gold Book 7

Father's Dream Book 8

Second Time Love Book 9

BAD BOYS OF SEAL TEAM 3 SERIES
SEAL's Promise Book 1

SEAL My Home Book 2

SEAL's Code Book 3

Big Bad Boys Bundle Books 1-3

BAND OF BACHELORS SERIES
Lucas Book 1

Alex Book 2

Jake Book 3

Jake 2 Book 4

Big Band of Bachelors Bundle

BONE FROG BROTHERHOOD SERIES
New Year's SEAL Dream Book 1

SEALed At The Altar Book 2

SEALed Forever Book 3

SEAL's Rescue Book 4

SEALed Protection Book 5

Bone Frog Brotherhood Superbundle

BONE FROG BACHELOR SERIES
Bone Frog Bachelor Book 0.5

Unleashed Book 1

Restored Book 2

Revenge Book 3

Legacy Book 4

Paradise: In Search of Love

Love Me Tender, Love You Hard

NOVELLAS
SEAL You In My Dreams Magnolias and Moonshine

PARANORMALS

FREE TO LOVE SERIES
Free As A Bird Book 1

Romance Book 2

Science Of The Heart Book 3

The Promise Directive Book 4

New Beginnings Book 5

GOLDEN VAMPIRES OF TUSCANY SERIES
Honeymoon Bite Book 1

Mortal Bite Book 2

Christmas Bite Book 3

Midnight Bite Book 4

THE GUARDIANS
Heavenly Lover Book 1

Underworld Lover Book 2

Underworld Queen Book 3

Redemption Book 4

FALL FROM GRACE SERIES
Gideon: Heavenly Fall

All of Sharon's books are available on Audible,
narrated by the talented J.D. Hart.

AUTHOR'S NOTE

I always dedicate my SEAL Brotherhood books to the brave men and women who defend our shores and keep us safe. Without their sacrifice and that of their families—because a warrior's fight always includes his or her family—I wouldn't have the freedom and opportunity to make a living writing these stories. They sometimes pay the ultimate price so we can debate, argue, go have coffee with friends, raise our children, and see them have children of their own.

One of my favorite tributes to warriors resides on many memorials, including one I saw honoring the fallen of WWII on an island in the Pacific:

> "When you go home
> Tell them of us, and say,
> For your tomorrow,
> We gave our today."

These are my stories created out of my own imagination. Anything that is inaccurately portrayed is either my mistake or done intentionally to disguise something I might have overheard over a beer or in the corner of one of the hangouts along the Coronado Strand.

I support two main charities. Navy SEAL/UDT Museum operates in Ft. Pierce, Florida. Please learn about this wonderful museum, all run by active and former SEALs and their friends and families, and who rely on public support, not that of the United States Government.

www.navysealmuseum.org

IF YOU GOT ANY CLOSER, YOU WOULD HAVE TO ENLIST

I also support Wounded Warriors, who tirelessly bring together the warrior as well as the family members who are just learning to deal with their soldier's condition and have nowhere to turn. It is a long path to becoming well, but I've seen first-hand what this organization does for its warriors and the families who love them. Please give what your heart tells you is right. If you cannot give, volunteer at one of the many service centers all over the United States. Get involved. Do something meaningful for someone who gave so much of themselves, to families who have paid the price for your freedom. You'll find a family there unlike any other on the planet.

www.woundedwarriorproject.org

CHAPTER 1

GRETCHEN HAD BEEN flittering around the dressing room like a girl readying herself for prom, Trace thought. Their daughter—his stepdaughter—Clover Sanders was getting married today. The sun was out, and the birds were chirping just like they always did, especially in April. Coronado was the most beautiful in the spring, but it didn't compare to his wife and how cute and flustered she was, sparking off expressions he'd never seen before.

"Relax, honey," he said, stopping her spinning by placing his hands on her shoulders.

She didn't make eye contact at first, but Trace insisted.

"It's going to be lovely, you'll see," he whispered to her, trying to sound super mysterious and sexy.

"Damnit, Trace. How do you stay so calm?"

"Because I will it so. Because I did 150 pushups two hours ago and a ten-mile swim in the bay before breakfast. I can feel my heartbeat against the leather soles of my shoes, honey."

She gave him that look, the one he liked, that tried to show him she was resisting him, but he was going to win the war anyway.

"And because I wasn't the one making all the preparations and coordinating everyone to carry out this mission. I'm just support staff. That's what I'm doing now."

As he expected, when he didn't release her and didn't stop trying to lock eyes with her, that smirk appeared and then bloomed into a beautiful smile.

"There's my girl."

"No longer a girl. I'm—"

"Perfect, in every way. Inside ..." He leaned forward, kissed her ear, and whispered, "Deep inside and outside. And you taste good too."

Her lips were soft and moist and demanded things of him he'd been already thinking about, but they didn't have enough time to execute.

"Better?" he said as he pulled back and studied her face.

"Much. Thank you."

"Oh no, thank *you!*"

She took his arm, and he escorted her to the narthex of the church, where they waited with the rest of the wedding party without the bride, the groomsmen looking like kids on a little league team but taller, Trace thought. He'd probably seen a bunch of them in their hot tub over the past several years, since most of them were long-term friends of Clover's as well as Jack's, her husband-to-be.

Jack was nervous as hell and kept smearing down his hair, which had been unfortunately over-oiled. It still didn't keep his wayward locks from shooting out like he'd stuck his finger in an electrical socket.

"I passed out at my wedding too. Not recommended," Trace said to the wide-eyed boy who was going to be his precious daughter's better half and was barely shaving. The kids were getting younger and younger these days.

"Mr. Bennett, sir, I wish you wouldn't talk like that, because, well, I keep seeing visions of me peeing my pants, shitting myself, or passing out. My odds aren't good, so I don't need to hear that."

"Just kidding. You'll be fine. This isn't the end of life; it's the beginning of life, son. You're gonna look back on it and laugh. Trust me on that."

"Mrs. Bennett didn't tell me you passed out."

"No. I meant my first marriage. And I should have been scared with that one. It was my body's way of trying to protect me. But I was punch-drunk on love or sex or a bit of both. It took time, but, when we finally got to know one another, we didn't like who we were together. It's different for you and Clover. You've known her—what?—seven or eight years?"

"Actually, almost nine. I was in her first class in Coronado when they all moved down here to be with you. We met that day and have been friends ever since."

"See? I was right. This is just about saying your lines in front of your friends and relatives. Nothing about the wedding itself should cause you any fear at all. You're a match made in Heaven, and, if I couldn't see the love with my own eyes, I trust Clover's judgment. I'll bet she worked you over and made you beg, am I right?"

Trace smiled internally, already knowing this to be true.

"That's putting it mildly. But she's worth it. I used to think she was trying to push me away."

"It's a trait of the women in their family. Want to make sure you're a keeper."

Jack mumbled agreement, searching the crowd nervously.

"They signal her when you are all inside. Don't worry. You won't jinx it, son."

Jack gave him a nervous laugh. "Mr. Bennett, I was wanting to talk to you about something. Could you help me get into a BUD/s class? I'm thinking of trying out for the Teams."

"You talk to Clover about this?"

"Sort of. We—"

"Son, you need to learn that you don't need my permission or help. You need Clover's. You find out if you got her in your corner first, and then you come talk to me, but not before. It won't end well if you do it the other way around. Women don't like to be second."

"But lots of your teammates joined that way. They just joined and made the grade."

"Because they weren't married. It's not like taking a few extra classes at the junior college, son. Whole different world. It will change you. Clover has to be on board."

"Understood."

Gretchen had been coordinating some things with the photographer and came over to Trace and Jack.

"Ready? The music has changed, and they say we can begin. Jack, go escort your mom and then come back for me, okay?"

"You got it, ma'am." He burrowed through the crowd and took his mother's arm, and they entered the church.

Gretchen sighed. "So young."

"I was thinking the same thing," answered Trace, his arm around her waist. "He's a straight-up good kid."

"I agree. And she's gonna boss him around like

crazy. Hope he's ready for it."

"If she's half as bossy as her mama, he'll love every minute of it."

He saw her sneak a finger under her eye to wipe away a tear.

"You're the most beautiful woman here, Gretchen. I knew the first time I saw you that you were a prize and just the right person to make my life worth living."

Kate and Tyler slipped in front of them with their youngest, Kendall, dressed in hot pink with a large, white bow at the top of her head, and her two older brothers steps behind. Kate waved, and Tyler punched Trace in the left arm as they quickly were ushered into the church.

Jack came back for Gretchen, and Trace sent her off with a kiss. His coloring was much better now, and, with the walking, he didn't look so pale and exuded more confidence. One by one, the other bridesmaids and groomsmen escorted each other down the aisle, turned, and waited for Trace to bring down Clover. They were stunning, the girls in shades of pink and rose, to the men in the Navy who wore dress whites. The other three wore white tuxes.

Minutes passed, but she didn't appear. As the music began again, Trace knew that Gretchen was going to be beside herself. Things could always go wrong. Although not a "runner" as some of his Teammates discovered occasionally, anything could happen. Could she have been kidnapped? With the way the world was, anything was possible.

He flew to her dressing room. With the phone to her ear, she sobbed. Her face was red and she'd smeared her eye makeup.

"Who is that, Clover?" he said as he wrapped his arms around her and pointed to the phone.

"It's Dad," she whispered.

"From prison? He's calling you from prison? That f—" He stopped himself before he uttered his favorite word.

"Look, Dad, I gotta go now. Trace is here and it's time. Thanks for calling, but please don't worry about me. I'll be fine."

Trace could still hear Tony's voice on the other end of the line when she disconnected the phone.

"Come on, Front Row. Let's get you straight. Everyone's waiting." While they hurried to the narthex, he asked, "What was this business with Tony? Why did that asshole—sorry, Clover, but that's how I think of him—get you so upset on your wedding day?"

"Trace, it's nothing. He's getting out soon, you know this, and he wants to spend time with me and Jack. Telling me all the things he wanted to do to make up for—"

And then Clover stopped and broke down and began to bawl.

Trace flew into a panic. If only Gretchen was here to make everything right. After all, as a Navy SEAL, he wasn't trained for *this* stuff. Ask him to do a snatch and grab, blow up a building, or stop a caravan of bad guys from entering a village? That he could do. But try to cheer up his stepdaughter at her wedding when her asshole father called from prison and victim shamed her, making her sad she had such a loser for a father? That wasn't something he'd trained for. That's what Gretchen specialized in. She'd know exactly what to do.

He grabbed her and hugged her tight, tighter than he'd ever hugged her before. He suddenly wasn't sure if he wasn't the one who needed strength.

"If I could take it all away, sweetheart, you know I would. But that's just the way things are. Life sucks sometimes. Sometimes the people we expect the most out of let us down. They treat us wrong, like your dad, and you still gotta love them anyhow. But it sucks. Just know, two hundred people are here who love you and can't wait to help you celebrate this beautiful day. This is your day, not his. He shouldn't have even called you."

"I know, but he's weak. He can't help himself."

"Right. And I'm going to be the gatekeeper until your mother tells me I'm wrong or going too far. No one is going to hurt my big girl. So you get yourself all cleaned up, just a little—"

He pulled out a mirror and handed it to her. Clover winced and nearly began crying again. With some of the supplies still in her hand, she worked on the makeup streaked under her eyes.

"The redness is already going away. Honest, honey. But they're gonna scream at me if I don't get you out there into the narthex. So help me out, okay? Help out this poor Navy SEAL from getting hit with a baseball bat by all the women here today, including your mother!"

"Oh, Trace. You're the best. I'll defend you." She giggled, dabbed powder on her face, threw the cosmetics in an offering bowl at the back of the church, and grabbed his hand. "Let's go kick some ass and take no prisoners."

"That's my girl."

IT WAS A beautiful ceremony, and the love that surged between Clover and Jack permeated the lovely April early afternoon, infecting the audience and wedding party with warm thoughts and magical wishes for the perfect life and union just beginning. Within seconds of the bride's appearance, her dress made of bright white satin covered in a sheer overcoat with pink butterflies and small pink rosebuds appliquéd and adorned with beaded pearls and crystals, the audience was stunned and immediately forgot the delay. As she walked, snickers rippled through the audience as they saw her favorite pair of volleyball shoes, died pink with hot pink laces.

The whole outfit was created by Clover and reflected her originality and her quest to celebrate life in all its forms. She clutched his arm and stood tall, bowing to the audience as they passed the aisles.

He savored this gift Gretchen had given him when he married her, because he never would have been able to walk a daughter down the aisle without her three beautiful girls. They were his, just as if he'd fathered them himself. He loved them all with everything he had.

The reception, even though he'd asked his teammates to keep it close and respectful, got a bit out of hand. A couple of the single Team Guys got drunk, one nearly getting into a fight with a Navy regular who was on the arm of a female guest, a friend of Clover's. Someone spiked the punch, and it had to be removed from the children's table, replacing it with another nonalcoholic punch. After that, someone made a store run for juice boxes and sodas, which were also consumed by the adults.

Some of the *Dancing with the Stars* type behavior was a bit risqué, lots of thighs and cleavages showing. People danced he never knew could dance, even with some stumbling and falling on the dance floor. It was always the same, whether the team was in full dress uniform or more casual. There was always the chance someone would embarrass themselves or someone else, but nobody got hurt, except for their pride.

The dinner was catered by the ladies auxiliary to save money, and the crowd stayed until the wine ran out. That had been done on purpose.

On the way home, Gretchen was exhausted but smiling, even giggling.

"I'm glad you had a good time, Gretch."

"Your buddies never disappoint. Those friends of Jack's came, the ones who just graduated from BUD/s. Nice boys who look you in the eye."

"They have no idea about the rest of the training. Deer in the headlights, my dear."

She smiled. "It must make you proud, seeing all these fine, young men going off to support and defend our country. You suppose Jack's thinking about that?"

"Like I told him, he better get Clover's permission first or he'll learn a very hard lesson."

She softly laughed. "Well, it's up to them. If he was my boy—"

"Well, he is, in a way," Trace interrupted.

"True, but I'm leaving it up to Clover, regardless of how I feel." She gave him a sexy smile. "You were most handsome, Mr. Bennett."

"Why, thank you, Mrs. Bennett."

"What do you really think about Jack going into the Navy?"

"Like you said, it's up to them now."

"Hard to see how he'd get veterinarian training becoming a Navy SEAL."

Trace laughed.

"What's so funny?"

"Oh, he'll get to work on, and with, some animals all right. Of the human kind. But if he's called and he uses his head, he could do it. It's all up here," he said, pointing to his temple.

"Oh, but, my love, you're so wrong. It's all in here," she said as she held her palm against his heart.

Trace moved her hand down into his lap.

"I like your ideas, Trace. And with Angie staying over with Mom and Dad, we'll have the whole house to ourselves." She kissed him on the cheek and tried to slide over closer, the gear shift getting in the way.

"I better hurry or I'll be banging you in the Walmart parking lot, sweetheart."

"That suits me just fine. But not under a street-lamp, please."

CHAPTER 2

G RETCHEN THREW HERSELF against the closed front door of their house when they returned. She hadn't recovered from their little tryst in the parking lot. Her head was spinning, and her breathing was still labored.

Trace's relentless lovemaking made her knees fold every time she thought of his determination to wring every last drop of energy from her. He demanded her full participation and then gave her complete satisfaction and more. Now ten years older, instead of being softer and gentler, he was even more driven and fully charged up, powered by his passion for their life together. It was impossible to resist him, and she never wanted him to stop.

He turned around, pulling her off the door and into his arms.

"That was fun. We should do that more often," he whispered.

Somehow, she drew up the energy to chuckle as she fell against him. "I'm beginning to think your first wife sent you away because she couldn't handle you anymore, strange as that thought is. How in the world did that woman let you go?"

"She tried to come back, remember?"

"Oh, yes, I hated that."

"I wasn't interested in the least. You know that's not who I am." He kissed her and, again, that sharp sizzle shot down her spine, making her heart race. "First time was a mistake. Second time, I hit the bull's eye. I mate for life."

"You just might kill me with your libido, Trace."

"Not a chance. I'm still waiting to love you hard enough to put another baby in your belly."

"Trace, I'm too old. I'm on the pill. You know this."

"Go off it. I want to make you pregnant. I want another little girl, but I'll take a boy. Maybe twins. Maybe one of each. Twins run in my family."

"Oh my God! Trace! You devil! That's not going to happen. Soon enough, you'll be holding your first grandchild, but we have to be patient with them. It will happen in time. That's going to have to be enough for us now …"

"I want more."

He began kissing her neck again, his knee pressing between her legs, making her quiver and ache again as she rode him. Even though she still had tender spots from their acrobatic lovemaking in the back seat of the Hummer, she was getting turned on all over again.

He abruptly stopped and spanked her rear.

"Go shower, and let me make some food to soak up all that alcohol. Then we'll get some nice rest and wake up lazy, but still horny, in the morning."

"Now I'm beginning to understand what my life will be like when all the girls leave."

After a long, deep kiss, he whispered to her lips, "Absolutely. Release the Kraken!"

He sent her off with another spank, and she laughed all the way to their bathroom, shedding clothes along the way. A good, warm shower would be good for her, she knew. It might help with some of the swelling and bruising she might have in the morning. Hummers were small spaces in the back, and the upholstery was rather unforgiving.

As the water sluiced down her body, she mused how exciting it had felt, like she was twenty again, and how her life had changed these last ten years, making the previous ten disappear—with the exception of the joys of birthing all three of her girls.

She rubbed her belly. Was there room for another in there? Would she be pregnant the same time as her daughter, Clover?

The answer to her query was *yes*. With Trace, all

things were possible.

She dried her hair and slipped on a robe, cinching it at her waist. She could smell Trace's specialty wafting from the kitchen: hot scramble, which was eggs with salsa and lots of cheese, stirred quickly in tablespoons of real butter. This would be followed up with pan-fried French bread slices and fresh jam from the farmers market.

He pulled the chair out for her and took obvious note of the gaping wound that was the front of her robe, raising his eyebrows and giving her a low growl as he bent over to serve her up the hot midnight snack.

"You smell and look lovely, my dear."

"These eggs look fantastic, Trace. I had no idea I was so hungry!"

"I noted you didn't eat anything but a donut and coffee all day. Not good for your body, Gretchen. We have to keep you in fighting strength." He growled again.

She laughed. "I thought I did pretty well tonight. I was able to keep up with you."

He sat down next to her and watched her eat. "You definitely did." And then he just continued staring.

"What?" she asked.

"I meant it when I said I want to make a baby with you."

"Trace, we're practically grandparents' age. Don't

you think we should act like it?"

"You mean I can't do this?" he asked as he slid his hand down her front and squeezed her right breast. "Oh, man, and no more of this?" He bent and sucked her nipple into a hard peak. "I want to taste you all over. I think grandfathers do that. Not in front of the kids, though."

"Aren't you going to let me eat?" she whined as he kissed her neck. "Or were you making this lovely food just to take it away from me?"

"Absolutely not. I just don't want you to forget what—"

Trace's cell phone rang.

"What the fuck?" He peered down at it and they both read: "A—hole" on the screen. "What the fuck does Tony want from us? He already ruined Clover's day."

"What? I didn't know about this."

He held his finger up. "Tell you later," he murmured before, "Hello, Tony. What can I do for you now? You out of toothpaste or condoms?"

Trace put it on speaker phone so Gretchen heard the profusion of swearing coming over the line, plus some background crowd noise.

"Same at you, man. Can I make your day worse, Tony? Just name it, and it will be incoming, special delivery right for you in a pail filled with dog shit."

Again more swearing. And then Tony began to sob.

That got Trace's attention. He sat up. "Tony? What's going on, man? You okay?"

"Like you care one thimbleful of jizz for me."

"It was your fault. You punched me first and you scared the crap out of your daughters."

"Shut up!" Tony yelled over the phone, which got a reaction from somewhere else in the hall outside his cell. "I need help, man. I need protection."

"Sorry, bud. No can do."

"Not here. I need you to protect me when I get out."

"The way I hear it, it's more dangerous inside, with all the gangs and the guards not making enough money for the danger they're exposed to. And my commitment to your family doesn't include protecting you, inside or out."

"I got people after me."

"But you're such a nice person, Tony."

"Shut the fuck up. I've only got another thirty seconds. I need you to pick me up on Friday when I get out. I'm supposed to get some money to some people that day."

"I see, so I need to drive you to the bank. Can't you take a cab?"

"You don't get the problem, you SEAL jerk-off. I don't have the money."

"I didn't realize toothpaste was that expensive. Are you using that many condoms?" Trace was having way too much fun and hadn't been watching Gretchen. Her anger began to boil.

Leaning into the phone, she asked him, "Who do you owe money to and how much?"

"There's this group called The Organization. They funded me an attorney to help with my appeals, and I signed with them so they could get me back on the court roster."

"That wasn't smart, not after nine years. You been practicing?" Trace inserted himself.

Gretchen put her hand over his mouth and frowned. "Tony, how much? We don't have anything we can give you."

"You can sell the house in Portland."

"That's your house."

"I owe more than the house."

Both she and Trace gasped.

Tony continued. "When the agency thing didn't work out, and it still might, but I thought I could earn some money with some of my gambling talents, and I lost. I lost big. Took a couple of bad chances I shouldn't have, and—"

Trace was holding his forehead and shaking his head. He made the gesture to Gretchen, his forefinger across his neck. Gretchen had to agree. Tony jumped in water so deep he was probably going to drown, his life ending over his bad decisions.

"I'd say more than a couple. Look, Tony, first thing you have to do is to get real with yourself and us, if you expect any kind of help. I can try to keep you safe, but you're not coming to live with us, and I can't protect you twenty-four seven. You'll have to raise the money. You'll have to negotiate time, and that might cost you something, probably more money. But you're in a spot, and, if you don't start telling the truth, you'll not only end your life, but you could endanger your family's as well." Trace was stern, deadly serious, and he wouldn't look Gretchen in the eyes.

"I understand," Tony said, drifting off into a whimper.

Gretchen shook her head from side to side, but Trace said it anyway.

"I'll be up there on Friday. We'll talk. Not going to promise anything, but I'll meet you as you walk out of there. The rest is going to be up to you."

The phone went dead, running out of time.

Gretchen knew Tony also was out of time. She feared this was going to have an effect on their whole family, and, with Trace being the protector he was, though he disliked Tony as a husband and father, he couldn't stand anyone who bullied people who were not capable of fighting back.

It was just his nature.

With a sinking feeling, she knew she'd never be able to talk him out of helping out the father of their daughters, for their sake, not Tony's.

CHAPTER 3

T RACE LANDED IN the Eugene Airport and rented a car, driving to the West Oregon Correctional Facility, a whole hour ahead of Tony's scheduled release time. He wasn't nervous about the visit, but he was concerned for the precarious position Tony had put himself in and how that would impact the family.

Gretchen had tried to talk him out of going, but he knew matters would only get worse if he ignored Tony, possibly spiraling out of control. That might be something no one could solve.

The facility looked more like a hospital. While gated and fenced, it was considered a minimum-security prison. All the same, psychiatric patients were housed there as well, and Trace knew that the criminally insane were probably even more dangerous than some of the hard timers in the maximum-security prisons. Their reactions were extremely unpredictable, and they could go for years on end without incident, suddenly having a crisis.

He'd promised Gretchen that, if Tony was a complete mess, he would try to deliver him to the proper authorities and get back home. He didn't like leaving Gretchen and the two girls alone. And he was missing out on greeting Clover and Jack when they got back from their honeymoon at the end of the following week. But if it took a week, Kyle had given him permission to handle it.

He parked at the main entrance, in front of the gate, but got out of the car and paced. A young woman and her infant were also waiting. The area looked more desert than the usual green of Oregon, even in April. The ground had been mowed extra short and had dried. The waiting lot itself was graveled with a light spray of oil, like he'd seen in the highway dividers for weed control. He heard occasional hawks overhead, but the nearest tree was more than a mile away, closer to the small one-church towns along the highway, just outside of Eugene.

He'd been told prisoners were never released early, but sometimes an hour or two later than their scheduled time. He checked his phone for messages and considered giving Gretchen a call but decided against it. He needed to wait in the desolate silence of a place no one wanted to be, and he didn't want to project any of that on Gretchen. He'd call her later, once he met up with Tony.

Retired SDPD Detective Mayfield, a friend of all the Coronado SEAL teams, had told him, "He has the option of staying in a halfway house. They're more set up for former drug addicts, but compulsive gambling is an addiction. He probably should try to get into some place like that for his own good, but most people don't take to it very well. It prolongs the stink of detention, and, as soon as they're out, they want their freedom. It's not a good idea, but that doesn't figure into the calculation, Trace."

Trace knew Tony wanted to stay in his old home in Portland, overlooking the river—the house Gretchen and the girls lived in alone after the divorce. His former lady was long gone after his conviction, so he'd probably live alone.

"He can't come here, Trace," Gretchen had told him. "I don't want him anywhere near the girls, and I don't care what he promises," she'd said.

"I understand, honey. But, as far as not seeing the girls, we may not have the clout to make that happen. If he wants to come to San Diego and is granted permission, he'll be on probation for a while, but we may not be able to do anything about visitation if he keeps his nose clean. I'll do my best, though. First things first; we got to get this financial thing off his back."

"Agreed. Have you made contact with the realtor in Portland?" she asked.

"No, that'll be my first call if that's what he's thinking." He asked her if she thought highly of the lady who sold them the house in the first place.

"Well, it was years ago, before we were married, and she's still in business, so I suppose she'd be the logical choice. But I don't know if she's followed things and knows what is happening with him."

Trace figured it would be hard to miss. He was sure all the local papers would be filled with the tall tales of Tony Sanders, wunderkind-turned-devil. "I'll check her out, and, if Tony agrees, that's probably also something we'll do—put the house on the market. Do you have any idea what it's worth?"

Her answer was quick and a bit nasty. "It's not worth anything to me. I don't even want to look at it. It's probably a mess, since I think he's rented it out to some tenants. I'd say six, seven hundred maybe? I really don't know what the market's all about."

Tony was released a hundred yards from the last gate. Trace clenched and unclenched his fists and said a little prayer.

Here goes nothing. Come on, Tony. Be a man and make it easy for me. I don't want to be here anymore than you want me to see you this way. Let's get it over with so we can all move on with our lives.

He remembered, when Gretchen kissed him good-bye, her message was brief, but stirring.

"Please be careful, my love. Come back to me soon. But watch your back. Nothing in Tony's world makes any sense or is very safe. Proceed like you're walking into a war zone; then, if you don't come under fire, you'll be pleasantly surprised."

I got you, Gretchen. Don't worry. It'll all be fine.

Tony's tall and now beefier form still had that cocky swagger he used to have years ago when he was actively playing ball for the Trailblazers. Trace figured he'd probably practiced some, maybe showed off a bit, but being incarcerated for these years didn't do anything to dampen his ego or his cockiness. That was a bad sign.

His sweatpants were brand new and baggy, and he wore high-top tennis shoes, not professional athletic shoes. He'd tucked his laces into his shoes and they had come undone and sloppy looking. He had on an oversized grey sweatshirt that was probably also prison issue, and, though it was huge across his chest and belly, the arms were about four inches too short.

All 6'6" of Tony reported behind the secure yard fencing. As if called to attention, his chin defiantly raised to the heavens, squinting at Trace and waiting for the gates to slowly roll open.

He slung his bag over his shoulder to the tune of

the tired, old wheels carrying the gate, stepped up to Trace, and stuck out his hand for a shake.

"Thanks for coming, man. I know this was probably one of the last things in the world you wanted to do, but I just want you to know I appreciate it. You're a stand-up guy, Trace."

"That's all right. We all make mistakes, Tony. What matters most is what we do with the rest of our lives. And you still have a lot of living to do. Besides, I didn't do it for *you*, and I think you know that. I did it for Gretchen and the girls."

He gave a "huh" in answer and then spat to the side.

"So let's get you set up, and let's see if we can move some mountains and get you started on a firm foundation."

"You able to bail me out?"

"Hell, no. I told you that already."

"Just checking to see if things had changed."

It pissed Trace off that Tony still had that cocky attitude after he'd thought perhaps the ex-convict was on a different trajectory.

"Look, I'm not able to contribute a dime to your care, but I can accompany you. But you're going to have to earn yourself out of this hole you've dug yourself into. I'm just here for—well, just consider me an Uber driver, okay?"

Tony shrugged, which showed Trace a lack of respect, surprising him slightly. He would've thought Tony would've been more contrite. But then he had to tell himself this was Gretchen's fucking ex, never a wise man and never able to control his emotions or his actions. Brilliantly talented, he'd still ruined his chance at a multimillion-dollar basketball career that could have set him up for life. That was going to weigh heavily on him as the days and months progressed.

The bigger they are, the harder they fall.

"Do you have to make a call to set up a meeting?" Trace asked him as they headed for the car.

"Already done. I got to go stop by a place down in the university district. There's supposed to be a bar this guy, my contact, owns. They passed me a message inside. I'm supposed to go there and schedule an appointment with some asshole who is expecting me to walk in with a wad of cash."

Trace was concerned about the setup. "You didn't tell anybody on the inside about your lack of funds, did you?"

"Not really. My cellmate knew, of course, but I don't think anybody really cared about what was going on with me. And I was limited to what I could do on the phone, so whatever calls they heard, they didn't hear anything about that."

"Well, you were pretty agitated when you talked to

me a couple of days ago. If they heard any of that conversation, then there are a lot of people who know, Tony. Remember what I told you? You got to stop lying to yourself. You're in grave danger if you're into some bad people for a lot of money. Want to tell me how much it is?"

"Well, let's just say it's more than the house is worth or more than the equity I have in the house, but I'm hoping he'll give me some time."

Trace noted that Tony still wasn't coming clean. And, again, he was disappointed and knew there was another red flag waving in the wind waiting for the war to begin. He hated situations like this.

"So we're on to Eugene?" he asked.

"Yes, sir. It's called the Red Hook Cafe and Grill. Someplace downtown, the Hippie District."

Trace put it in his GPS, and it found a location, indicating it would be twenty-five minutes to arrival.

Tony turned in his seat to face him. "So how's the happy couple?"

"Well, they've made it to Hawaii. Sounds like Clover really loves it there. They've got a condo overlooking a golf course on the rainy side of Kauai."

"I know it well. It's a damn good golf course if it's on the North Shore."

"I wouldn't know, but they seem to like it. It's rained every day so far, but they're having a ball. Of course she talks to her mother more than me, but Jack's a good kid, and I think he has the cojones to make a good life for her."

"Well, that's good. I hope that maybe I can help them. If I can get onto a semi-pro team—we call 'em 'G League'—I might be able to earn a little bit of income, do some coaching maybe. First I got to get this jerk off my back."

As Trace drove down the highway and then turned off to the signs of Downtown Eugene, he asked Tony about how he got involved in gambling behind bars.

"Prison's got TVs. They've got ways of betting on games. I mean, that's all we do is watch games, because the classes are shit. I'm never going to fucking learn how to take apart a motor or cook. I don't want to learn how to bake bread or peel carrots, for Christ's sake. The only thing I like to do is read magazines and watch the sports games. We were not really restricted so it was easy to make bets, even though we couldn't do it online, so the fees were high, and payout was difficult."

"Yeah? How do you handle that?"

"Two ways. First, you can get your wife to bring in some for conjugal visits, but you took care of that, Trace."

"Like I said, this isn't my rodeo, Tony."

"Other way is more expensive. The pros do it the

second way."

Trace thought to himself that, of course, Tony thought he was one of the pros. And that nearly told him the whole story. Tony's ego wouldn't let him NOT gamble like a pro. They nailed him on that, Trace suspected. He'd fallen for it, and it would cost him.

"The pros, you gotta be worth something to do the deal this way. Gotta settle up after you get out, and that brings with it a whole other set of problems. There were also protection scams. Some guys were worth a lot of money if they paid out in the end. You get in with somebody and they protect you, for a fee, so you don't get knifed before you pay."

It hurt his heart to say it, but Trace couldn't resist.

"Sort of like the honor system, except with ridiculous interest rates, right?"

"Yeah, you gotta be approved for it. Only a few get that plan. If somebody was worth a lot of money but of course didn't have it, there could be things done on the outside to pressure them to pay up. It's a big racket just like it is anywhere. More dangerous though. The guards, they all knew what we were doing, and they didn't care really. As long as nobody got hurt."

"And how long did it take to rack up this huge bundle you won't divulge? I take it that it's more than the cost of a new Bentley?"

"Well, I was doing pretty well there. I was actually a

couple hundred thousand ahead, but, all of a sudden, things changed in year four when it looked like these guys were able to secure me a spot on one of the eastern amateur teams of a big club. There was going to be a signing bonus, which would give me plenty of money to live on for the next few years if I was careful. All of a sudden, I started losing, and that bonus, if it ever really was there, got eaten up in less than a year. I think they saw me as a paycheck."

"Tony, that's always the way they treat you. Those guys always see suckers who bet on their games as paychecks. They win more than they lose. That's how come it's so lucrative. And people will take a chance at things when they're desperate. I'm sorry you didn't get some counseling or some help with that. Don't you have an attorney? A probation officer? They should have intervened."

"Story of my life, Trace. That was one thing my last coach told me just before I packed up my locker. He told me I would've been a much better player if I would've listened and been coachable. Hell, I played more basketball than that guy ever did and he was twice as old as I am. But I do have a habit of kind of learning my own way."

Trace turned off the highway toward downtown, noting how much seedier the stores and shops and houses looked the closer they got to the university.

Protest signs were common on front lawns or draped on hand-painted posters hanging from the front porches. Unlike most of San Diego, the young college-age students dressed in colorful clothing with brightly colored hair, elaborate tats, a variety of piercings, and all sorts of styles. It was almost déjà vu for Trace, who had seen pictures of San Francisco during the Haight-Ashbury times, and this reminded him of those photos he had seen in an old Life magazine.

They pulled up to the Red Hook Cafe and Grill, and he accompanied Tony inside. The interior was so dark Trace wished he had night vision goggles to flip on, and he paused a couple of minutes to let his eyes adjust. A lone guitar player sat on a small stage in the right-hand corner of the dive. Hardly anyone in the audience in front of him was paying attention and— this being the middle of the afternoon—more than likely the spectators wouldn't improve until after dark. Tony sauntered up to the bar and asked the bartender his question.

"I am supposed to ask for Sam. I guess he's the owner of this place?"

The bartender nodded as he polished a shot glass and set it down. His face was bright red with a bulbous nose that screamed alcoholic like a neon sign.

"You guys want something to drink?"

"Not for me, thanks," said Trace quickly.

But not Tony. "Sure, this on the house?" His cocky manner hadn't been turned down one notch.

"You got to be fucking kidding me. You're here to see the boss and you're asking if it's on the house? I don't know you from anybody. Your money's as good here as anybody else's. It will be ten bucks for a beer, for you."

"Ten bucks! That's robbery."

"Well, that's because you kind of dissed the owner. Better not do that around here very much. These guys bite. When you were inside, didn't anybody teach you any manners? You don't go walking up to people in the box and treat them like that. Why would you do that here?"

"I'm sorry, man. I'm new to all this."

The bartender nodded his head and gave a smirk, then studied Trace, and angled his head back, examining Tony again. "I said you better be careful. These guys bite. You don't want to get bit by these guys."

Tony looked at Trace. "Can I borrow ten bucks?"

And so it began. Trace pulled out a twenty and handed it to Tony, who handed it over to the bartender. He got a light beer on tap, and the bartender didn't give him change.

"Mmm," Tony said after he took a sip. "The best fucking beer I've ever had."

Trace was going to have to have a talk with Tony.

He was going in all the wrong directions and pissing off all the wrong people. He nudged Gretchen's ex. "Can I have a word? Let's take your beer over to the corner. I need to talk to you." To the bartender, Trace said, "I'll have another beer for another ten, and I'm sorry, sir, but there's no room for a tip."

The bartender handed Trace his light beer on tap, his face expressionless.

Trace thanked him and asked, "And are we going to be meeting this guy, Sam, or what's the program here?"

"I already messaged him. He'll be on his way ... ten, fifteen minutes maybe. You just go have a seat. He'll find you."

Trace headed to the opposite corner from the singer so he could give Tony some advice, if he was up for it.

"Tony, the bartender's right, and you're taking offense before you're even engaging. Remember that, when you're walking into battle, the enemy gets a vote. It's their territory. They know what they're doing, and they already have a plan and a strategy. You're walking into something, and you don't know what you're walking into, so you can't afford to be cocky or piss off somebody. So you better just swallow your pride and get with the program. Otherwise, you're going to get yourself in worse shape than before. There's a limit to what I can do. And I will not be dragged into your shit. As much as I want to help you for the sake of Gretchen and the girls, I'm not going to be mired in your mess. So don't do that anymore, or I'm out of here, and you can find your own way home, wherever that is."

"I just didn't like him taking advantage of us."

"It's not the greatest injustice in the world. You have to pick your battles carefully. You understand?"

Tony nodded.

"Why do you think they wanted to meet you here? This is their turf. You have no say in the matter. You gave up all your rights when you overextended yourself, when you paid them their ridiculous fees, when you agreed to pay them back and couldn't control yourself from losing more money. You gave up your rights. You have no rights here. They're letting you live. They're letting you in their establishment so they can fleece you some more. So, get ready. Because that's what they're going to do."

"How do you know so much about these people?"

"Look, Tony, I've seen evildoers all over the world. They don't change their stripes. They don't start out being assholes and then all of a sudden get real nice and reasonable. They get worse. So it's not to your advantage to piss them off."

"I just don't want them to think I'm afraid of them. They don't scare me."

"Well, now you're being downright stupid. Don't you remember that phone call you made to us? You were scared out of your pants. Don't sit there and tell me you're not afraid of them. You should be afraid. And, if you're not, you're even stupider than I thought."

"I just think I've got a certain amount of pride left. I got big plans to turn my life around. I just don't want them to think they're dealing with some spineless creature that is like all the other losers they work with."

Trace started to chuckle, shaking his head in disbelief. "All they deal with are losers, Tony. And you're at the top of the list. You're the biggest loser of them all. You gave up an NBA career, for what? What was the payoff for you so you could do it your way? So what are you going to do if they decide, okay, you can't pay us back? Maybe we'll just take a couple of your fingers or take your life or maybe hassle one of your kids? Have you ever thought about that?"

"Yeah, I've thought about that. I am not going to let that happen. I'm not complete scum."

"I want to believe you. I really do."

Trace and Tony exchanged a stern study of each of their characters. What Trace saw in Tony's eyes was total capitulation. He wondered if he had some kind of a suicide or death wish. And did that mean that Trace had just gotten himself in one hell of a mess?

"You just keep control of your emotions, Tony. If you think you have to show some of that bravado, sit on it like a fart when you're out with a pretty girl instead. Just be quiet, and let them do the talking. After we know what the plan is, then we'll know how to react. You're going to want to get the house on the market right away, and we should get up to Portland and do that. The sooner you can get them something, the better, and you're going to need some money to live on. You got anything else you can sell, liquidate?"

"I got a Bentley convertible, but it's been in storage all this time. Hasn't been run. I might be able to get seventy or eighty thousand for it. It's a sweet little machine, or it was."

"Okay, they set you up with any retirement plan or anything like that on the team?"

"No. Most of that went toward my legal fees. When I was done with the trial, I didn't have much of that left, and I was docked some early penalties, and I still owe a tax bill, but they've given me forbearance until I'm out."

"How much do you owe the IRS then?"

"It's about a hundred. Hundred and fifty maybe now."

Trace glanced at his side. How could one man so singlehandedly mess up his life by accident? No, Trace thought, this wasn't by accident. It was on purpose.

Tony was on some kind of death mission, and that meant he was extremely dangerous.

"Well, first, we find out what's the deal here, and then we make our plan. Do you know this guy Sam at all or some of his colleagues?"

"No, they had a whole board of directors at the prison. I only worked through them. They told me Sam would get me hooked up with who I needed to talk to. I don't even know what this guy looks like."

Just then, a heavyset gentleman who wasn't more than five feet tall walked into the bar. His shirt opened one button too far, revealing a gold coin encrusted in gold filigree hanging around his beefy neck. He wore cowboy boots, which made him look like a small pixie, not a cowboy. His blue western-style shirt matched his jeans. But he did have an expensive haircut and fresh shave, and he headed right for their table.

Tony stood up to shake the man's hand, and Sam motioned him to stay put.

"You stand up like that, son, and I'll shoot you right there. That's an aggressive action. I kill people who do that."

Trace knew he was dealing with a pure amateur.

"So don't do that to me. You sit. Now, how much money did you bring with you today?"

CHAPTER 4

GRETCHEN AND KATE gathered at a restaurant to have breakfast, sending off their parents. Mr. and Mrs. Morgan lived in Palo Alto up north, and it was a long one-day drive for them.

"It was such a lovely wedding, Gretchen. You should be proud of yourself," said Mrs. Morgan. Her husband, Joe, seconded that.

"I've never seen her look so beautiful, sweetheart. She was just glowing. She looked like she'd been out in the sun, had a nice tan on her face," he added.

Gretchen knew that was from all the crying that Trace had interrupted shortly before Clover walked down the aisle. But she wasn't going to reveal her daughter's secret.

"I really think they'll be happy, Mom. Jack seems like a wonderful guy for her. He's going to be okay with her being headstrong, sometimes negative at times. She works hard, and so does he."

"What's this I hear about him perhaps wanting to join the Navy?" asked her dad.

Kate turned and stared back at her. "Oh my God. I didn't know that. Is that a real thing?"

"Well, I guess he discussed it with Trace, but, hey, you guys aren't even supposed to know about this. We don't even know if Clover has been asked, so we certainly don't want to create a scenario where the whole family knows it before she does. If she doesn't agree, both Trace and I will counsel him that he shouldn't go. But, if he enlists, we'll give them our full support, so all we can do is wait."

"She told one of her bridesmaids that her dad called her before she walked down the aisle and apologized for not being there," whispered her mom.

Gretchen shrugged, trying to appear casual about something that bothered her a great deal. "Yeah, well, we've had years to get used to that. Now he starts wanting to hang around, when he needs something. He's due to get out soon, and, well, it's just not going to be easy for all of us. So pray for us, Mom and Dad, please. Please pray for us."

"You got it, kiddo. Any of my cop buddies in Palo Alto, I'll let them know about it too, because if he's going to be hanging around your family at all, I'm going to let them know he's not to be trusted. I still don't trust him, and I don't think I ever will." Joe's face darkened with concern.

"It's not for me to say," Kate began, "but you and Mom taught us about forgiveness. And when we can, we should."

Gretchen knew her mother would react negatively to that and wished her younger sister hadn't mentioned it.

Louise stiffened her back. "No way. There's forgiveness, and then there's being stupid about it. I think we'll never trust him. You might forgive him, but I would never trust him to be alone with the girls. Surely, he isn't going to request that, is he?" Louise asked her.

"I don't think so. And, of course, being a convicted felon, there's no way he would get full custody or even partial custody. It's going to be supervised visitations, if anything at all. Of course, that's assuming the girls want to see him. Angie might a little bit, because she was quite young when all of this happened and he was sent away, but I don't think Rebecca would. And Clover, well, she's got Jack now, and I'm pretty sure Jack wouldn't like it either. So I think we're okay. It's Angie I probably have to watch out for the most."

"Hey, where is Trace anyway?" asked Joe Morgan.

Gretchen looked up at Kate before she answered. "Actually, I should have told you to begin with. He's gone up to Portland to help Tony get situated. He's being released today."

"Oh my Lord, just when I thought everything was going to be smooth sailing for a while, this little thing gets thrown in," her mother complained.

"Well, that's kind of why Trace is there. I mean, who else in the family could handle it? And, apparently, there are some loose ends that Tony needs to tie up. He owns the house outright, so he'll probably have to sell it and possibly sell some other assets as well to have money to live on. I doubt there'll be a chance any team in the NBA, even a nonprofessional training club, would take him. Maybe he could get a coaching job somewhere if it didn't require a background check, but anywhere on the West Coast, that would be difficult. Still, there's always a possibility someone would give him a chance somewhere. Perhaps a private school coaching job or athletic director. He does have a college degree and was well thought of in the day. Had quite the following. He would make a good coach. But the rest of his life is a hurricane. And I don't think it's getting better."

"You think he'd learn his lesson, that knucklehead," said Joe.

"Well, they always say 'you can lead a horse to water but you can't make him drink.' He had all these years to think about what he'd done and to try to make amends with himself, other people, but he really didn't reach out much. I thought, at first, he was just embarrassed for his behavior and maybe a little bit irritated that I'd moved on so quickly, but I've come around to the conclusion he just doesn't have the capacity to be caring for anybody other than himself. And that's sad, because he wasn't at all the guy I thought he was or the guy I first met. Remember those days?" Gretchen asked the table.

"Oh, I was so enamored with him. This big, tall, handsome basketball player all the girls wanted to be around. Of course, later, I learned about all that happened," said Kate.

"Not to mention all his extracurricular activities and his gambling problems."

Gretchen looked at her father after his comment.

"You knew he had gambling problems way back then?"

"I heard a couple of my buddies talking about how he was doing some interviews for an online gaming platform, talking about betting on games, and he was sort of a spokesperson for some group that was trying to get subscribers. I just assumed that he was doing that maybe to pay off some debts. That's a lot of times what athletes do. And they're not supposed to bet on their games or professional league games of any kind, but he sure was into it. We know it's an addiction. He *looked* like a gambler to me."

Gretchen thought that was interesting and pondered it carefully. This would be something she wanted to let Trace know about. Perhaps the people involved in the online gaming were also the ones he bought from.

Louise Morgan slapped her husband on the shoulder. "Well, Joe, I guess we better be on the road. I'm stuffed to the gills. I said my goodbyes before Angie left for her game. And I said goodbye to Rebecca last night. I wish we could have stayed long enough to see Clover come home safely, but that's the luck of the draw, isn't it? Have her call your dad and me, okay? I'd like to hear all about the honeymoon. We also have a special wedding present we want to give them."

"Oh, thanks, Mom. I'll do just that. I don't think she's posting anything on Facebook, and Trace kind of schooled her on that—no TikTok either, not letting the whole world know they were young newlyweds on their own, but I'm sure she'll take lots of pictures and send them to you when she can. Don't worry, you'll see them. I haven't seen any either, but I have talked to her once, and she's having a blast."

"She was talking about snorkeling and doing some paddleboarding," Kate added.

"Yes, and she collects shells too. I know she's loving it. Away from Mom and Dad, they get to do the moonlight strolls down the beach, the little umbrella drinks out on the lanai. I have fond memories of Trace and I doing the same thing. But, of course, we weren't married then."

"Well, kiddo, your secret's safe with me. I don't know if you've told the girls all the details, but I ain't saying a single thing," said Joe.

"Thanks, Dad."

Kate and Gretchen walked them to their car, waving them off, and then left in Kate's car, heading to her house. They had about three hours before they had to pick up the kids. Kate's were at a birthday party for one of the SEAL kids who was new to the area.

"More coffee?"

"Oh, gosh, I'll never get to bed tonight if I do. I'll take some water, though."

"Coming right up."

The two of them sat in Kate's living room. She had decorated it with posters of Chez Panisse and other famous restaurants and little Parisian bistros she'd collected over the years. Some were truly vintage advertisements for restaurants long gone from all over the world. It was an eclectic and colorful room and reminded Gretchen of Kate's mother-in-law, Deirdre Gray. A well-known artist in Portland, most of her paintings had been destroyed in a fire in the Warehouse District several months ago, and they had moved down to temporary quarters in the Coronado area.

Kate told her Tyler's parents would've been invited

to the breakfast this morning, but they were taking a gardening course.

"Gardening? So they're learning that now?"

"Well, sort of goes along with our plans, Gretchen. A beautiful wedding center, gallery, and event location, like we talked."

Gretchen smiled at the thought of Deirdre and Mr. Gray getting on their knees digging out weeds and planting flowers. Coronado was a special place and very easy to grow things, even citrus and bananas. She hadn't had the time, but she fantasized about Kate's wonderful ideas of opening a catering business housed at the center.

"What are you thinking about? You're smiling. I'll bet you're thinking about Trace," said Kate.

"No, I actually was thinking about your in-laws. Looking at the walls of your living room, I could almost feel Deirdre's presence here even though they don't live in this house. Can't wait to see what they find."

"I know. We are kindred spirits. And you get along with her too, right?" asked Kate.

"She's so much fun. I don't think I've ever met someone so full of life, and she wears her clothes and her big beads and jewelry and her hair things like she's a walking canvas. I'm glad to see she's moving on, and I really think she'll be a good partner for your little venture."

"I want to make sure you're okay with all of this, because I don't want to do this without you."

Gretchen frowned.

"I don't know how good I am at all this stuff, but I'm certainly willing to help. I mean, you usually want partners for two things, first for their money, and second for their talents. I don't think I have either of them."

"That's not true. I think you have a very good business sense, and I always run things by you that are financial. Gretchen, you know that. I trust your judgment. You read people really well. You were the one who warned me about Randy, and then you warned me about getting involved with Tyler before my engagement was over with Randy."

Gretchen nodded her head. "Yep, and, as for me, I made my choice, and he was the first person I fell in love with, and Tony was a total dud. Nice at first, but he turned out to be a wolf in sheep's clothing. Trace was only my second boyfriend. I don't shop around a lot, do I? Is that a good thing?"

"The best. You are an excellent study of people. And you know who the good ones are. I'm so happy you met Trace."

"And he came along at just the right time too. God love him. I never expected to fall in love again or to fall in love so hard. He says the same. Second time love is the best."

"No arguments from me. Oh! I almost forgot! We took Deirdre's VW van, and I found a little upholstery guy here who does wonderful things to the interiors. We made up a color scheme, Deirdre and I, and she drew out what we thought we'd like to have the interior look like—the cabinets, how the kitchen would work, place for seating and food prep. We have to install a stove, more like a griddle, storage for supplies, a refrigerator, and tiny all-in-one bathroom. We have a lot to do to meet current food selling standards. If we were just keeping it private, we wouldn't have to do so much. But look at these."

Kate showed Gretchen some of the sketches Deirdre had done for them. The cute little Volkswagen van with the ten light windows on top was outfitted in the drawing with yellow and white polka dot curtains. The interior appeared a beautiful blush pink color with light-stained cabinetry. The outside of the van would be repainted a very pale green. It all looked very fresh and sporty, and it suited Kate's energy and her ideas.

"This is what your bedroom looked like when we were growing up, remember? Same colors and everything."

"I know!"

"These are fabulous. You have any idea how much

it will cost?" asked Gretchen.

"Well, hopefully, it won't be more than about fifty. Tyler thinks it'll go higher, but this little guy is going to give me a really good price. He does custom seating arrangements for restaurants with his signature tuck and roll. Works restoring old cars too. He's sort of a car buff, and most of the local car collectors hire him to restore interiors for shows. He's quite famous in the industry."

"What a find."

"He's very busy, but he kind of likes the idea of working on a food truck. I think he'll probably get business off it. Who knows? We could be opening up a new type of collectors' car! 'Food Truck Specials,' we could call it. What do you think?"

"Wow, I bet his shop is just awesome. It would be fun to see his work."

"No, not awesome at all. It looks like a typical garage mixed with a tailor shop, scraps of leather and leatherette all over the floor. He's got about ten tables and several full-time seamstresses, plus one apprentice he's hoping will take over his business someday. He has enough for someone to work full-time just maintaining the leather sewing machines and the other equipment they've got."

"I'm impressed."

"They are patenting a stamper, so they can do embossed work, and also a pattern cutter, instead of having to hand cut everything. But right now, except for the stitching, which is all done with machine, most of the rest of his work is done completely by hand. And he can custom do wood framing and detail work on the inside as well as metal accessories on the outside. Deirdre came up with the idea of a bumper in the back that highlights the name of the food truck."

"I can't wait to see the vision. You've got a winner there, Kate."

"I think the guy's really, really talented. He told me I should get a bigger van, so Tyler and I have been looking at old plumber's trucks, utility vans, you know, the kind that have built-in shelves?"

"Oh, yes. You know Mom used to tell us about Edy, the vegetable man, who used to come down the street and sell to all the housewives back then. His truck was painted up in bright boho decorations. The fruits and vegetables were all boxed in colorful little crates."

"I don't remember those stories. It was probably before my time. But I wouldn't be surprised."

Gretchen checked her phone. "I think I need to go. Friday traffic."

"Hey, Gretchen, let's go look at spaces when you get free. Let me know. We can pick up Deirdre and do a little girl exploration. How does that sound?"

"I could use some distraction right now. That

would be fun. Do you think Deirdre is free today?"

"When will Trace be home?"

"I'm not sure. Supposed to call me tonight."

"Maybe Angie could babysit over here while we go?"

"I'll ask her. I'm sure it would be okay. Her schedule with her practices and coaching the little ones is pretty full, but I don't think she had plans today. I can ask."

They hugged before each making a call. Gretchen knew she was going to go to bed tonight with colorful images floating around her brain, probably keeping her up way past her bedtime. But it would be a welcome distraction to replace the worry in her heart with the chance of such a colorful future.

CHAPTER 5

T RACE DIDN'T TRUST one hair on Sam's body, and
he had a lot of hairs to choose from, even protrud-
ing from his nose. His beefy presence was not menac-
ing as far as people went. He was used to seeing
oddballs on deployments, but there was just something
about the man he didn't like or trust. Not that Trace
would ever like any of Tony's friends. Sam seemed like
the type of guy who would just as soon steal your food
as rip you open with a knife. He was that casual about
the way he dressed, about the way he talked. Plus,
everyone around him exhibited fear, which told Trace
he'd probably done his fair share of murder and
mayhem, and he wasn't anyone to fuck with.

"So who's your asshole friend here, Tony?" he
asked Tony.

Trace noted that he talked to Gretchen's ex as if
he'd known him for a long time.

"Sam?" Tony asked, caught off guard.

"No, fucking Santa Claus, you asshole. I asked you a question, and I want an answer. Who the hell is this guy?"

Trace started to speak, and Sam cut him off with a hand to the face.

"No, I said him. I want you to tell me, Tony."

"This is my ex's new husband. This is Trace. Trace meet Sam."

"No, I said who *is* this guy? Like who *is* he? Who is he to *you*? It ain't right that you're hanging around with your ex-wife's new boyfriend or husband or whatever he is. I need an explanation, Tony."

"I brought him for backup. I didn't know what I was running into here. Trace is a member of the military. He's a Navy man." Trace was glad Tony didn't mention he was a SEAL.

Sam looked him up and down but didn't ask him to stand. Of course, he noted Trace's tats on his forearms and then peered with dark, beady eyes right into Trace's. These types of men often measured bravado by whether or not he blinked, so Trace decided to let the guy off the hook and blinked early. This wasn't the time for a show of strength. That seemed to satisfy Sam that he was dealing with someone who wasn't as violent or dangerous as he was, and he liked that thought.

That made him very, very dangerous.

"So, Trace, you packin'?"

"No, sir. You can check if you like."

"No, thanks. But don't try anything here. So, Tony, I guess, has told you about his little situation?" He finally sat down at the table and turned toward the bartender, summoning him over.

"Yes, sir, what would you like, gentlemen?" the bartender asked after he scurried over.

"I'll take a whiskey," Sam said. He gestured to Trace and Tony.

"A whiskey will be fine for me too," said Trace.

"You can make that three," Tony added.

"Okay, so we have some numbers to throw out, my calculations are somewhere in the range of $950,000. Is that about what you came up with?"

Trace whistled in spite of himself. After all, any normal person would have the same reaction, and it didn't seem like a good idea to pretend that that chunk of change was easy to get.

"Holy shit, Tony, you didn't tell me it was that much."

Sam blurted out, "So you're lying to your friends too? You lie to your ex? I know you lied to the guys inside. I had to pay off some of them. They were damn angry you didn't pay up."

"I couldn't. Everything was tied up."

"Well, now you're out, and now you can be of use

to me. You are going to get me the money. Let's talk about that, the important stuff."

"Well, here's the thing, Sam. All my money is tied up in the house. I have a few things I can sell, but I don't know how much the house will get, but it's free and clear, so I'll sell it and give you whatever I can get."

"Okay, so that's going to take three or four months. That's longer than a hundred days, right?"

"What's the hundred days?" Tony asked.

"It's what you promised my committee in the joint. You can't do that?"

"I can get you maybe fifty thousand, go get a line of credit, and bring you that in a few days, I think. I don't think I can get you more than that, because I'm basically unemployed, and I'm a felon, and I don't have a job."

It was the first time Trace saw that Tony was actually telling the truth.

"Okay, so you think you can get me the fifty grand within a week?"

"Yes, sir, I do."

"If you don't, you're going to lose a finger. I'll let you choose the finger, but I don't think it'd be a very good idea for you to be minus a digit if you're planning to play any kind of basketball ever again, do you?"

Trace saw Tony's face go completely white. "I'm a man of my word, sir. I'll get you the money. I should be good for it. There's tons of equity in the house."

"And because you're not paying me within a hundred days, unless you can do that, the interest is twenty percent a month, so in four months, five months, six months, you're going to owe a hell of a lot more than 950K. What are you going to do for the rest?"

"I have no means of earning income. Teachers or coaches, they don't pay anything, and I can't get a job in a regular school because they don't hire felons. I'm all ears. I can work for you if you like."

The bartender brought over the whiskey, and Sam's face lit up with delight. He threw his back in one large gulp and slammed the glass back on the table. He clapped his hands together and rubbed them, smiling with a huge Cheshire-type grin. "Now we're talking, I've got some special plans for you. So we keep on this schedule, you get me that fifty thou by … I'll give you ten days, okay? After that, it starts getting bloody. I don't like bloody, especially in my establishment here, but, after you get the house on the market and you get an offer, I want to see what you're going to be netting, and I want to make sure you give me all of it. I don't have to tell you that it's in your best interest to get the house sold quickly. We'll see what's left afterwards. I don't want to promise right now, but I've got some really good ideas how you and I can make some money."

"Is it legal?" Tony asked.

Trace sipped his whiskey and squirmed. He knew, of course, it wasn't legal. And it was only going to entrench Tony further in this guy's clutches.

"Sam, if I may?" Trace asked.

"No, but go ahead anyways."

"Is this money owed to you? What guarantee is there that he pays you off and someone else doesn't come after Tony for the money. Do you have something that proves it's your debt?"

"You obviously don't do this for a living, do you?"

"Obviously."

"The reason it's my money is that I'm gonna kill him if he doesn't deliver it. Now, does that clear things up for you?"

"Partly. If he pays you off, then he's free to go, no strings?"

"Where are your brains? He's done when I say he's done. You see, I'm the aggrieved party here. He's shown me no respect. If he plays by my rules, he gets off, but not until I say so. Now, if you don't mind, don't ask me any more fuckin' questions."

"It's okay, Trace," Tony mumbled.

"So now you're standing up for him? Tony, we're going to have to have some serious discussions about protocol. Or, maybe your ex wants this guy to get you shot. Did you ever think about that?"

"No, she wouldn't—"

"Jesus Fuckin' Christ. I think you're about the dumbest motherfucker I've ever met. Wake up and smell the coffee. The whole fuckin' world's for sale. You can do anything you want as long as you pay the price."

"Okay, got it."

"So back to whether or not it's legal. That's in the eye of the beholder. May not be exactly legal, but it'd be pretty hard to prove. You've got a lot of information, inside information about trades, and you got friends still, I'm sure. Some of that information leaks out, some of that information could be useful to me as far as placing my bets."

"Sam, I've been out of the game for a number of years, and none of my teammates have ever visited me. I'm pretty sure they don't want anything to do with me."

"Well, you're going to have to try then. You're going to have to try to make the rounds, see what you can find out about your old team. And, in a way, it's reasonable, because you're looking for a job, right? Ask your old coach if you can be the ball boy for Chrissake."

Trace rolled his eyes. He knew instantly it was a mistake.

"You've got a problem with that, Grandpa?" Sam

asked him.

"You mean, do I think it's likely that a professional basketball player could turn around and be the ball boy for the team he used to play for? Is that what you're wondering about, Sam? I thought you were smarter than that." Trace knew he had to keep it light, but he just couldn't help himself.

"I see your friend has more sense than you do. So we'll find something for you to do, but I want you to get back into someone's good graces on the team. Maybe not the Portland team, maybe Sacramento, San Francisco. I don't know. I just want inside information, and that's how you're going to pay off the rest."

"Sounds kind of nonspecific. Can you give me any details?"

"You wearing a wire or are you just stupid?"

"No wire. Like him, you can check."

Sam stood up, and, for a second, Trace thought he was going to slap Tony across the chops. He took a turn, inhaled deeply, and then sat down, folding his hands in front of him on the table.

"We have a problem, unless you wind up with a sugar daddy who gives you all the money. Then we don't have a problem. You pay, you stay. You don't pay, you are permanently retired, and painfully."

Sam looked over at Trace. "I'd be kicking myself all over the place if I didn't ask. Are you his sugar daddy,

Trace?"

"No, sir. I'm on military pay only, no side jobs, and my wife doesn't work. We're supporting one in college and one going to college. There's no money in my family to donate to this cause."

Sam scratched his beard, winced a little bit, and nodded his head, thinking. "I got you. I like your style, Mr. Military Man. I think you and I should talk some more about our futures together."

CHAPTER 6

K ATE, GRETCHEN, AND Deirdre spent the afternoon pouring over some of Deirdre's plans for a space she and Kate had discovered in a warehouse district close to the beach where new recruits for the SEALs traditionally trained.

"I love the idea that we can grow lots of beautiful gardens—flowers, flowering trees, veggies, and herbs— and also host wedding receptions inside or out that take place on the beach since it's so close," said Deirdre.

"It's really a perfect spot," Gretchen agreed. "I've driven through that area."

"I see festive and decorated golf carts and open-air buses shuttling guests to and from," said Deirdre. "The space has two stories, and, with a tilted roof, you have some really nice light coming in during the day or starlight for evening receptions. The walls are perfect for displaying paintings and other artwork. It's a painter's dream!" she added.

"I'd like to take a look if you've got time," Gretchen said.

Kate was enthusiastic for the idea. "Let's do that. And I'd like to show you what our little upholstery guy has come up with. We thought it would be kind of cute to have a soda fountain and ice cream store at the east end, set up for kids' parties and fifties-themed events. We'd have connected music boxes on the tables in booths with plastic padded seats in all the ice cream colors. He made a mock-up of one of the booths and several tables bordering in a retro metal trim, making it look just like an old-fashioned soda fountain. I can't wait to show it to you, Gretchen," said Kate.

The three ladies arranged for Angie to babysit Kate's younger ones and then took off on their adventure. Sunday mornings on Coronado were always mood-enhancing for Gretchen, and it was no different today.

Just as it had been described, Gretchen saw a long, warehouse-type building that even had a grain elevator on the inside, which she noted could be fixed up to serve customers on both floors since Deirdre had designed the interior so there was a second-floor ring that rimmed the building on the inside.

When she stepped farther inside the nearly five thousand square foot space, through the double glass doors, it felt like walking into a church of possibilities. "Listen to the acoustics in here. Boy, you could do some musical events that would be outstanding."

Deirdre gestured up. "From the second floor, if we add some side windows and doors and maybe a few small balconies on the outside just big enough for a couple of tables and chairs, you can actually see the ocean from the building. That's a million-dollar view from up top," said Deirdre, pointing to the ceiling.

"There's your way up," Gretchen said, pointing to the metal basket elevator standing near the wall on the south side. "You could design some wonderful metal sculptures for that thing," she mused.

Kate jumped in. "This being a steel structure, there's nothing in the middle to interfere, and no structural walls would have to be built. We're just talking about interior walls for the kitchen. Perhaps we buttress them against the elevator, add a classroom or demonstration kitchen, and make a place for storage as well as an office. We even thought about putting in an apartment upstairs for an office manager or caretaker at some future date. You and Larry could live here temporarily if you wanted to, although it's not the size nor the scope of what you're used to, but it would work for temporary."

"I like that idea, if we can get out of our lease. I'll see what Larry says. I love living inside my art. It's the *only* way to experience it!" she answered.

Kate demonstrated where they considered putting the soda fountain and booths, a sanded concrete dance floor extending the entire length of the building, which would expose the aggregate pebbles, enhanced with color. She indicated where the killer sound system would be housed, along with a small stage for performances. On the west side, with added windows and doors leading out to the patio and gardens, it would be perfect for sit-down dinners, wine tasting, and afternoon wedding receptions.

The more Gretchen looked at the space, the more excited she got.

They continued around the building as Kate showed Gretchen the property lines extending back nearly two hundred feet. "There's room for parking, and the lot to the back is also available."

"Amazing," was all Gretchen could think of to say.

"I'd like to put in some raised beds and grow our own vegetables," said Kate. "Maybe eventually we could have a cooking school here, but this area would be great for the catering trucks, getting them under a carport system that would also support solar panels. And the raised beds on sprinklers would allow us to grow all our herbs and vegetables for the business, maybe even set up a retail country store, even get a fruit orchard going, although that will take some years to develop," she squealed.

Gretchen gave her bouncing sister a hug. She hadn't seen Kate this excited since she'd discovered she was pregnant years ago. "I can see it all just as if it was finished. What a beautiful space and concept. When do you put the offer in?"

Deirdre shrugged. "It's in the insurance company's hands now. The adjuster is getting ready with his final numbers. Once we know what we have to work with— and we've already received some of the funds for our living expenses down here—but once we know for sure, then we'll know what we can offer. The property's been for sale for over a year, and there have not been any interested parties, so I think now is a good time to jump on it."

Gretchen noted the neighborhood was very tidy, especially for an industrial district with mostly existing cinder-block buildings painted with colorful murals built during World War II. At that time, arched ceilings, Quonset hut type open truss-beamed build- ings were the style, and several had been car dealerships at one time. But now, most of the struc- tures were light manufacturing or industrial companies occupying them, small operations that needed the space for production and storage. One of the neighbors was a wholesale nursery that sold palm trees and other tropical citrus and greenery.

Further down the road was the infamous flesh skin graphics, the tattoo parlor Kate said most of the SEAL Team 3 guys went. "It has a dubious reputation, of course, not sure if you've heard, sis."

That made Gretchen curious. "Single SEAL stories?" she asked timidly.

"Sacred ground. They have good memories of those days, as it should be."

Gretchen had an idea. "I think if you're able to buy the building and start the business, we should choose a logo and all of us get a matching tattoo maybe on our wrist or forearm somewhere. What do you think about that?"

"Like the guys do on SEAL Team 3," Kate agreed.

"Well, I don't have one yet. I guess, once you get over seventy years of age, it's about time, right?" said Deirdre.

"I love the idea," said Kate. "That's going to be your job, designing the logo. What should we call it?"

"Bone Frog something. Has to have that in the name," Gretchen suggested.

"Bone Frog Art and Garden Center?" added Deirdre. "But I think that's too long."

"Bone Frog Center. Just keep it simple. You could do a spin on the bone frog logo, maybe put flowers on her head … has to be a her," added Kate.

"I see T-shirts in our future," said Gretchen.

Next, they visited Jose's upholstery shop, which was on the other side of Coronado, a little bit north of the base. Also in an industrial district, instead of light manufacturing and commercial storage units this area was filled with auto body shops and engine repair and overhaul auto repair shops. It was not a particularly good part of town, unlike the warehouse they were considering purchasing. But it was a car-lover's haven with dismantled vehicles, including abandoned school buses, trucks, and classic clunkers just about everywhere they looked. For those who loved collecting and tinkering with old cars, it was truly paradise.

Jose greeted them as they walked through the roll-up door into his kingdom. He was wiping his hands on an oily rag.

"*Buenos días, señora,*" he said to Kate.

"This is my older sister, Gretchen, and you already know Deirdre, my mother-in-law."

Jose held up his dirty hands and begged off shaking theirs but greeted them with a curt nod. He motioned for them to come to the back of the shop.

"As you can see, I made a demo of your booth just so you could get an idea of the space and the colors I can do. I made it as a sample using all different colors in pastels on one side and the bright colors on the other side. I wouldn't make it this way, of course, but this is just an example of what you can have."

He pointed against the wall at a colorful booth with bubblegum colors on the right and bright fluorescent colors on the left, meeting in the middle, making a U.

"All it would need is a retro Formica tabletop. And we can attach it if you wish, but I think it's better that you can move it around. That way it's more flexible if you want to make an area for dancing."

Gretchen's fingers smoothed over the plastic upholstery, loving the richness of the texture and the colors.

"Jose, this is fabulous. It looks like something out of an old diner. You're quite a craftsman."

"Well, this is kind of fun for me, because most of the time I'm restoring old vehicles, and I have to use material that looks like the original, and much of it is with drab colors. With these, just like with custom hot rods, we can kind of go crazy. That's the real art of it all."

"Please show my sister the drawings of the van, how you're going to fix it up," Kate asked him.

On the wall over the upholstered booth was a blueprint of the insides of Deirdre's van, done in blue scale, but Gretchen could see where the cabinetry, the bathroom, and the kitchen were located.

"I'd like to put a pop-up in here; that way if you take this somewhere you have to travel, someone can sleep on top. The health department won't allow you to sleep downstairs in the kitchen. But if it's a separate pop-up area that's temporary, they will allow it."

"Good to know," said Kate.

"I've found some old panel trucks and utility vehicles that might work. I'd like to find something that needs total work," he said as he waved his hand through the air. "We put a new engine in it, we completely redo the insides, and I make the outsides open with a canvas canopy that can be locked down at night. That way, if you have things you want to sell, like food supplies or drinks, it can be a regular food truck but not like any food truck you see around here. I think, with more space, you'd have a better kitchen, and you could hold more products. You wouldn't have the bathroom, of course, but we can put in bigger refrigeration, make the drawers into coolers, and perhaps have some of them hold ice water. In Mexico, my cousin kind of patched together one of these, and he's going to send me some pictures. I'll show you later."

"So these are the trucks you were talking about, Kate?" asked Gretchen.

"Yes. But I think we should start with the van first. Don't you agree, Deirdre?"

"It all depends on the numbers." She addressed Jose. "Do you have any figures yet?"

Jose shook his head. "No, señora, not yet. I am just swamped this week, but maybe next week I'll have an idea. The nice thing about your van is that it's stock, already works, but you may find that if you use it much, you're going to need some upgrades to the motor."

"Oh, yes, that thing's a slug when it comes to hills," Deirdre agreed.

"With the cabinets we'd be putting in, it's going to make that worse. Quite a dog going up any hill. So you might want to consider getting more horsepower. But I understand your concerns about cost, and we will give you prices both ways."

"Thank you. That would be helpful. We aren't super rich, so cost is probably our most important element. I think everything else we can negotiate, even the price of the building. I'm hoping the sellers will be flexible enough so that perhaps we would make up the cost of the upgrades to the vehicles with the savings on what we pay for the building," answered Deirdre.

Gretchen could see that Deirdre had a keen eye for bargains, and, with her experience designing and building her artist gallery and workshop in Portland, she'd learned from her mistakes and was going to be using all that knowledge to benefit the project here in Coronado.

Afterward, they stopped for a light lunch, and then Gretchen picked up Angie, and the two of them went home. Angie was filled with questions.

"I'll show it to you after they get it in contract, honey. Right now, it's just sort of a pipe dream. It has to be something that's affordable for Deirdre, coming from the insurance proceeds. But I think it's doable, at least it looks like it is, and it would be fun to work on. Might be a good little part-time job for you too," she said to her youngest.

"I would love it if Aunt Kate could show me how to cook and do catering. I have friends at school who work part-time for catering companies, and they make pretty good money. I think it would be fun to do that and save up for college."

"Absolutely, sweetheart. This is an opportunity that most kids your age never get. You wouldn't have to be going off to an expensive culinary school to get the kind of skills that Kate has already. She's fabulous, and she's wanted to do this for, well, ever since she was in high school herself. She ran the Heller's wine-tasting room, and two SEAL wives she's friends with do this up in Sonoma County. You've been there. But way before that, she first started talking about having a food truck. I know it's going to be a success."

After a brief pause, Angie asked, "When's Trace coming home?"

"I'm expecting a call from him sometime today. It doesn't sound like it's going to take too long, but you know how your dad is, and there are always surprises when it comes to Tony. I'm glad we have Trace to help him out."

Angie was quiet suddenly. Gretchen used the opportunity to speak on the subject.

"I'm sure he's going to try to spend more time with you girls, and it's really up to you as far as how much you want to see him. But he is your father, and we aren't going to make you do anything you don't want to do. Just understand that."

"Is he different, Mom? Like do you think he got better?"

Gretchen groped for a way to keep her language civil. She scrunched up her nose. "Well, I haven't seen him, of course, but Trace doesn't think so. He's the same old Tony."

Angie sighed and sank deeper into her bench seat. "He embarrasses me, Mom. Some of the boys at school tease me about him. I try not to pay any attention, but they laugh sometimes and call him stupid names."

"What kind of names, sweetheart?"

"Double Dipper, Fuzzy Balls Sanders, that sort of thing. Worse, too."

She wasn't sure how to respond, but, before she could, Angie asked her, "Did he really hurt Trace?"

Gretchen realized Angie was talking about the fight Trace had gotten into with Tony, one of her ex's wild and crazy, alcohol and drug filled events where he was completely insane and out of his mind. Gretchen knew the girls worried about their dad, and she was so grateful for Trace's presence to help calm the situation.

"I'm sorry, sweetheart. I think we'll have to take it one step at a time. Trace will give us a good report when he gets home. Hopefully soon. Before your sister gets back from her honeymoon. I would try not to worry about it too much, Angie. There's a lot of people helping to look out after you guys. Especially with everything that's occurred. You've seen more of the seedy side of life than most of your friends have. Unfortunately, some of these things aren't very pretty and you've gotten closer to danger than any of your school friends will probably ever be. But I know you'll take it as a learning experience, and I know you will grow and understand more and more what families are all about. I know we will forgive your father, but we aren't going to give him too many chances to put any of us in harm's way. That's what Trace has promised to do."

"I know. It's not fair that he has to do that, but I'm glad he's there. I think I love him more than Dad. Is that wrong?"

"I'm proud of you for being honest about that, Angie. It's a natural reaction to the love that he's bestowed on all three of you. He's a good man, and we're lucky to have him in our lives. Tony's lucky to have him help with this transition, even though I'm not sure he completely understands the gift. But we'll forgive him anyway and hope that, in time, he'll get better, and then we can relax a bit. Right now, we're going to be pretty vigilant and limit everyone's exposure to him. So, no texting, no computer messages, no calls that Trace or I don't know about. Okay, Angie?"

"You got it, Mom. Thanks for everything you do for us. I hope someday I can be just as good a mom as you are. And I hope I get to marry somebody just as nice as Trace is."

Angie's words warmed Gretchen's heart. She was going to love telling Trace about their conversation this afternoon.

CHAPTER 7

T RACE AND TONY traveled to Portland. On the way, they stopped by a branch of a bank Tony had banked with. They gave him applications to fill out and also showed him how he could apply online when he got home, if he chose to.

Tony wanted to stop overnight someplace, but Trace insisted they make it all the way back to Portland so they could spend the night in Tony's house. He needed to see what kind of a situation there was there.

"Well, I got tenants, and I guess I have to ask their permission before we can stay there. They could say no," Tony replied.

"Okay, we'll ask them, and, if they say no, we'll get a hotel. No problem."

Trace gave a call to Gretchen before they continued driving, just as it was turning dusk. He didn't have much to report and didn't want to report the few pieces of news he did have, because he didn't want to worry her. But he could tell from her reactions that she was concerned.

"Just wanted you to know we're on our way to Portland, and I got Tony. The rest are things we discussed about the house. I'll fill you in more later. I'll be driving until dark."

"Again, be careful."

He told her to give his love to the girls, even Clover if she talked to her, and then they said their goodbyes. He continued the drive to Portland, getting there just after eight.

Trace remembered the house that Gretchen and the girls had lived in, but he had never thought of it as Tony's house. Gretchen had said it gave her and the girls a nice stable place to live, and Tony had always promised the proceeds from renting out the house would pay for their college. Of course, that never came to fruition.

The house needed a lot of paint on the outside, and weeds taller than his waist reached for the night stars. He knew it would look even worse in the daytime. A couple of beat-up Volkswagens were parked in the driveway, blocking any route to the back entrance next to the kitchen.

Parking illegally in the street, he accompanied Tony up the steps to the porch, and they knocked on the front door. Heavy metal music blared from the insides.

As Tony's tenant opened the door, Trace was hit with a blast of smoke coming from inside the house. He turned his face away and swore, noticing the guy gripping a red bong in his right hand.

The young man was dressed in swim trunks and a dirty T-shirt. His long, blond dreadlocks were disheveled, their roots frizzing. His blue eyes were disarming but glazed over. He was very clearly under the influence.

"Can I help you?" He slurred his words.

"Hey, bud. Joel, is it? I'm Tony Sanders, and I own this house. You're behind on your rent, kid."

"Oh, really?" He scratched the back of his head, turned, and yelled to the rear of the house, "Hey, Nicole! Did you not send the rent in? I gave you the cash, didn't I?"

As a female voice shouted something in return, Tony added more information.

"Look, man, my records show you're behind three months, not one month, and I need a place to crash, and this is my house, and, since you're not paying, I'm going to stay here tonight with my friend here."

Joel put his hands up to his ears. "Whoa, whoa, whoa, slow down. I'm getting messages from both sides here. I can't talk to two people at once."

He studied Trace, and then lazily his gaze returned to Tony, who responded, "Yeah, I'm your landlord.

And I need to stay here."

"I don't like that guy. He looks dangerous." He pointed to Trace with a whine.

Trace pulled on Tony's arm. "Hey, man, we don't want any scenes. Let's just go get a hotel."

Tony, being Tony, wiggled himself loose and confronted the tenant again. It was another stupid move.

"Joel, you're an asshole. I got some pretty powerful friends who are real bad asses, and they'd love to just fuck you guys up real big. So you get out of my way, and you let me sleep on your couch or your floor or someplace, because I just got out of prison, and I don't have any money, and I don't have any other place to stay."

The guy raised his eyebrows on the opposite side of the screen door. That certainly did get his attention, although it wasn't something that Trace would've recommended anyone do. But it was having good effect.

"Hey, man, I'm sorry about all this shit. How about me and Nicole just take off for a day or two, and we'll come back after you found a place to stay? Will that work?"

Hallelujah, he's seen religion!

"So when you come back, I'm going to change the locks, and, if you don't have the money, you aren't going to be able to get your junk. Get your ass moving and get your cars out of the driveway so I have a place to park, and you come back when you've got the cash. If you don't have the cash, I am going to fucking find you, and I'm going to take one of your fingers."

Trace's spirits spilled into his socks. He'd allowed Tony to engage against his better angels, and now could see it was a total mistake. But he was also concerned Tony would just get amped up further if he tried to stop him. So he decided it was two against two, and he wasn't going to start a fight, but he sure as hell would try to protect Tony if one started. And he didn't want to do that either, but he was not left with any other good choices. Pulling Tony off the porch was going to be a bad move.

Tony was relentless. "I'll take that as a yes. But I mean it. Or I could take one of your toes, one of your big toes. I'll even let you choose whether it's the right foot or the left foot, asshole."

Trace leaned into Tony and whispered, "I think he got the message, Tony." He stared at Joel, who put his bong down and pulled his dreadlocks behind his ears, tying them together with a large rubber band. He was quickly sobering up.

"You've got about thirty minutes to get your stuff out, and we'll wait out here for a bit. We aren't going to touch anything of yours, but, if you call the cops, I think you're going to find that they will not take too kindly to squatters," Trace said.

Now Joel was getting defiant all of a sudden. "Oh, you think so? We don't have cops in this town anymore. And they don't care if squatters take over some rich guy's house."

Trace realized his mistake. He had to intervene, and he did so gently but with force in his voice.

"I don't think you understand. This gentleman is in a great deal of distress, and he's on a tight time schedule, reinforced by some threats from some very bad dudes, like he said. So you have thirty minutes, and then we're going to come in, and we're going to stay here, and I think we'll be done by Sunday, Monday at the latest. So find someplace, gather your stuff, and let us have the house. By the way, we are going to be putting the house on the market."

"Are you two a couple?" Joel asked.

Trace was beginning to lose his shit. Nothing about working with Gretchen's ex was turning out the way it was supposed to. Everything was harder than it needed to be, and he tried to remind himself about those little speeches he'd received his entire career about the enemy getting a vote. Now he felt like a goddamn fool for even volunteering for this failed or soon-to-be-failed mission.

"Look, asshole, I don't want to hear another word from you. All I want to see is asses and elbows, got it?

You get out of this house in thirty minutes, and you can live to play another day. Okay?" Trace tried to give him his most angry, wretched look, and it appeared to be working.

The door slammed in their faces, and they could both hear the tenant giving orders to the mysterious Nicole, who at first didn't believe him that they had to gather up their things and vacate the house for a few days. She argued with him until Joel brought her to the front door so she could look through the window at the two guys looming on the porch. That's when she got it. Her eyes grew large as fried eggs, and she soon disappeared. Next thing they heard, both clunkers in the driveway backed up, screeched tires, and took off down the roadway.

"God, I hope they didn't lock the front door. I don't have a key anymore," said Tony.

"Let me know if you need me to break the window," said Trace without a smile. He was tired, he needed to lie down, and he wanted this day to be over. He wasn't going to call Gretchen again tonight, even though he'd promised.

SATURDAY MORNING, THEY filled out Tony's paperwork, then took it into the bank. The pretty, young assistant manager indicated they would have an answer by closing time that very same day. When the loan was approved, Tony asked if he could borrow a hundred thousand dollars instead of just the fifty he'd applied for and was quickly told no.

"We'd like to help, Mr. Sanders, but this is all we can do. We hope that when you get back on your feet, you'll come back to having a deposit relationship with us. That's why we're helping in this time of need," Trace heard her say on the other end of the line.

"How do I get the money then?"

The young woman at the bank explained the money would be digitally deposited to his account on Monday. And three days later, the funds would be good.

"I'm not sure what my account numbers are, and I don't have any credit cards with me. Can you make me a new credit card?"

"Surely, Mr. Sanders. A debit card. That's a good idea. I can do that and have it mailed to your home in about ten days. How's that?"

"Not good enough. I need it quicker than that, and I need the loan proceeds on Monday. I can't wait to have it clear the bank."

"Well, we don't hand out that large amount of cash, but I can make out a cashier's check for you. Do you have a person's name you want me to make it out to? That way he or she can deposit it in their bank."

"Sam. That's all I got," said Tony.

The assistant manager coughed into the phone.

Trace interjected, "Listen, ma'am, if you put the funds in there digitally, is there a way you can make them good the same day so he doesn't have to wait the three days? And will he be allowed to pull the cash out right away? Or can he pull it out in stages, say over the next three or four days?"

"Excuse me, Mr. Sanders. Who is this person?"

"He's my …" He looked at Trace. "What do I call you?"

"Mr. Sanders, is everything all right?"

Trace cut in again. "Excuse me, ma'am, but I'm helping Mr. Sanders with getting his life back in order post-incarceration. I am married to his ex-wife. We are family in a way."

"I see. Well, let me check with my manager. Why don't you call me back on Monday and we'll see if we can make some kind of an accommodation for you? If I give you a cashier's check and it's not made out to anybody, it's dangerous to travel with such an instrument left blank. But perhaps we can request funds on special order. I'm just not sure it'll be available Monday. The easiest would be to deposit it to your checking account, and then you can write checks against it."

Trace could see Tony was getting irritated. It didn't bode well for his future that he couldn't even figure out how to access funds, get a loan, or work out details without Trace's help.

"I think that would be fine, right, Tony?" Trace said in response.

Having received the good news that his $50,000 was approved, the next order of business was to meet with the realtor they had called to visit the house this afternoon. Trace spent some time cleaning up some of the dishes, sweeping and vacuuming the floors, making beds, and trying to tidy up as much as he could, while Tony lay back on the couch with a cold, wet washcloth on his forehead, sporting a splitting headache, he said.

Trace figured the realtor would understand that, since it was a rental for several years, it might need some work, but, as they were in a hurry to get it liquidated, hiring people to do such a thing wouldn't be possible.

Shirley Ledbetter was right on time and held her diminutive, red fingernailed hand with the charm bracelet attached to her wrist for Tony to shake. He was nearly twice her size. But Ledbetter, from the advertisements that Trace had seen in his days visiting Gretchen in Portland, was an extremely successful agent and had a reputation for being no nonsense.

"It's nice to see you again, Tony. I'm glad that you called me. I think I have a couple who might be interested in this, depending on the price. Are you interested in something fast?"

"Hell, yes." He motioned for her to come inside and introduced her to Trace. They sat in the living room initially, and then she got up to do a quick walkthrough of the house without Tony or Trace hovering behind her. "I like to look at it the way a buyer would see it, not with you explaining things to me. I'm going to take some notes of things that maybe we should address, but I like to see it in the eyes of a potential buyer."

Trace was impressed, and they both nodded. He could tell that she questioned his presence, and, since Tony hadn't properly introduced them, he did so himself.

"Ma'am, I am now married to Gretchen, Tony's former wife. As you've heard, Tony's had a run of bad luck, and I'm here on behalf of Gretchen and the girls, to help him out a bit. Not financially, of course, but just to help him with the paperwork. He is in a bit of a financial bind."

Of course, before the agent could respond, Tony disagreed with Trace's opinion. "Oh, wait a minute. I've got money. No, we want to get the top dollar for this house. I would like to do a few little things so we can just really rake in all we can. So help me with this, Shirley. Okay?"

Trace worked very hard to control his anger again, already the second or third time today that he had to do so.

"Ma'am, that's not exactly true. He does not have a lot of time. As you know, he's been incarcerated."

Shirley quickly responded this time. "Yes, sir, I understand fully. And while fixing it up to get top dollar might be usually the best way to go, this couple who I have are young contractors, and he doesn't want to pay for somebody else's work that he'd have to rip out and redo anyway. So, in this particular case, the fact that we want a quick sale works very well for this particular buyer. He has all cash, and he's most anxious to find a place. They've lost just about everything they've tried to offer on."

"Okay, I'll let you do your job."

Trace sat back and let her do her walkthrough. Of course, Tony couldn't sit and wait for that to be over, so he got up and started explaining things to her, exactly what she told him not to do. Trace also heard him ask her for names of plumbers and electricians, painters, and people who could help spruce it up. He shook his head in disgust. Tony was never going to learn.

The two of them returned to the living room and joined Trace. "So, after seeing all of this, I think you can get close to eight maybe. This is a very popular part of town, it's away from the downtown enough with all the problems there, but it has the nice view of the river, and it's a close commute if people are going north to Washington state or south if they happen to work down toward McMinnville or Eugene. It's a lovely, older neighborhood, as you know, not a lot of rentals. I think if I explain to the couple that you've not lived here for several years and really hadn't been able to keep track of the tenants and the condition of the house, I'm pretty sure they will agree to take the house as is. But I am going to need to show them very soon."

"Sounds good to me," said Tony. "When?"

"Well, the good news is I'm showing them another property tomorrow morning early. Perhaps we could come over here afterwards? About 10 o'clock—or 11:00, if you need later?"

"Let's do 10:00. So how does this work then?"

"Well, I have prepared a contract for you, and I left the price blank until we talked. I would need you to sign this contract, and it doesn't obligate you to this particular couple, but it does give me the right to show the property and collect a commission. We can discuss a longer-term listing agreement if the two parties cannot agree. I did not prepare that."

Tony signed the single-party listing agreement with Shirley, and, as the two of them watched her navigate the creaky front stairs, her hand gripping the handrail on the left and her heavy briefcase slung over her right shoulder, Trace thought for the first time that perhaps this was all going to work out fairly quickly.

"Let's go grab some dinner. On me. Steak?"

"Sure thing, man. I could use a good steak. My cooking skills are shit."

"So are mine. On that we agree. Hey, I guess we're more alike than I thought?"

CHAPTER 8

GRETCHEN WAS INVITED to one of the SEAL Team 3 legendary bonfires, welcoming several new recruits to Kyle's squad. She went with Rebecca and Angie.

It was good to catch up with several of the other wives, many of whom had been present at Clover's wedding. She was rewarded with compliments and glowing accounts of how lovely Clover looked and what a great time they had.

Christy introduced her to Margarita Tamu, the wife of Isidor Tamu, both of whom were born and raised in Mexico and had been naturalized as citizens of the U.S.

"Margarita is also a gifted dancer and artist. They have three girls, just like you do, Gretchen," Christy let her know.

Gretchen shook the beautiful woman's hand. "So wonderful to meet you. Please, if you have any questions at all, don't hesitate to give me a call. I'm sure Christy has already given you the phone tree, and I'm Gretchen Bennett. Trace Bennett is my husband. I know how it felt being invited to my first one of these parties years ago, so I'd be happy to share my perspective on how this whole brotherhood thing works. Maybe you'll find some of it useful in navigating the society they've created here."

"Thank you. I would like that. You are very kind."

She was drop-dead gorgeous with an attractive smile and smooth accent while she spoke flawless English, with her "twist."

"Which one is your husband?" Margarita asked.

"I'm afraid he's not here tonight. He never misses these, but he's up in Portland helping a family friend." Gretchen felt the words stick in her throat.

"I understand."

"We can also share babysitting and other things as well. So don't be a stranger, and don't feel like you are bugging me, okay? It only feels intimidating at first. In fact, it's really very easy to get to know everyone, and, soon, you'll find a real family here. And if you have any trouble with the young, single guys who may not have the manners they should have, you let me know, and I'll have it fixed."

They both laughed.

"Thank you so much. Everyone is so welcoming

here. I was told of this, but it's very nice to see. I'm sure my Rosie, Camilla, and my Angie will very much enjoy meeting your girls."

Both Angie and Rebecca were presented to Margarita, and each shook her hand.

Christy had been watching from the side, checking something on her cell phone, pretending not to hear, but she stepped forward. "Well, I'll leave you together," she said. "Gretchen, would you mind introducing her to several of the other wives? I've got a little reconnaissance I have to fulfill for my husband."

"No problem, Christy. Happy to do it. Oh, and does she have the phone tree? I'd like to highlight my number for her. She can use it as reference as she meets people."

"No, I forgot." Addressing Margarita, she said, "I'll make sure to drop a copy by your house tomorrow, okay? It was stupid of me. My mind is tired."

"You and me both, Christy," Gretchen agreed.

"Everything go okay up north?" she pried.

"Yes, I believe so. Just that I think Tony is more of a handful than Trace was expecting. But I'll fill you in tomorrow sometime."

Christy walked off and cornered a new couple who had just arrived.

Gretchen leaned into her new friend and whispered, "Christy runs a tight ship and is the perfect complement to her husband, Kyle Lansdowne, the Team's LPO. If Kyle is the glue that holds the Team together, Christy is the wire frame it's attached to. She makes it a point to know everything about everybody on Team 3, better than her husband."

"I see. She appears very confident and kind. She commands respect, doesn't she?"

"You bet. None of the guys would ever cross her, or they'd hear about it from Kyle. They are a matched pair, a real team of two. You'll find that you can trust her. And do yourself a favor and take her advice to heart. It will be a lot easier on you both if you do."

"Do your girls play volleyball?" asked Angie, Gretchen's youngest daughter. "Because both Rebecca and I have played, and we both coach. We'd be happy to have your girls sit in on one of our clinics."

"Well, that's lovely. I don't know if they have ever played volleyball. My husband has been playing soccer with them since practically before they were walking. You know soccer is more popular in Mexico?"

"Yes, Clover and Rebecca played soccer. I didn't care for it," said Angie.

"Are they on a team?" asked Rebecca.

"Well, we're still exploring, but I understand the United Club is quite good. Both my girls would like to play soccer in college, and this would help with the costs. They are a little bit younger than you two, so they have lots of time before they have to think about that, but soccer and sports for women is very important, no?"

Rebecca immediately answered her. "Oh, yes. Clover and I both received partial college scholarships for our volleyball. Soccer is also very big."

"I think it's good for women, because they usually recruit more for the soccer teams than they have to for any of the other teams. Maybe softball as well, but, for soccer, the teams are huge. In Mexico, sometimes they have a bench of thirty or forty girls. They have difficulty finding enough fields and coaches, so their teams tend to be very big."

"Well, you're going to have to bring your girls to one of our clinics. If they give it a shot, they might find they enjoy volleyball." Angie asked, "Are they tall?"

Margarita threw her head back, her beautiful brown curls flashing in the night air. "Oh, no. We are small packages. Very powerful, but small in stature."

Gretchen couldn't resist adding, "Good things in small boxes."

Everyone laughed at that.

Later, there was an announcement by one of the new recruits, Roger Valise—he and his girlfriend Vanessa were now engaged. Gretchen thought they looked even younger than Clover and Jack. She took Margarita by the arm and introduced her to Armando.

"Armando is from Puerto Rico. My husband has nicknamed him the Latin lover."

"Well, Gretchen, in all fairness, I haven't been single more than a few months in decades." He greeted Margarita warmly. "Actually, they call me Armani. They think I spend a fortune on clothes, but I buy them at the discount stores. Very nice to meet you. I hope you will enjoy our little community."

"Thank you."

Gretchen added, "Armando remarried last year. His first wife was killed on the job. She was a policewoman. Lovely lady."

"Yes, Sambra sends her regrets, but we shall have to call on you some time and get properly acquainted. We have one child, Artemis, and we're always looking for new babysitters, if you have daughters of the right age."

"I have three. My thirteen year old loves babysitting."

"Wonderful. Sambra is also relatively new to the group. She'd love meeting you, I'm sure."

He said his goodbyes and wandered off.

"It's quite a lot to take in, and I'm sure you'll have questions. But, culturally, it's very important that the SEAL wives be included in the work. They are part of the job," Gretchen said as she brought Margarita over to Libby Cooper.

"I've heard about this. And I've heard about how

the group stays together, how they help each other through good and bad times. I am so very proud of my husband. He always dreamed of living in the United States and working for the U.S. military. As a boy, he was fascinated with stories of World War II and Vietnam. When the opportunity came up for him to begin citizenship by applying for the Navy, he jumped at the chance. He's not regretted it since."

"Welcome, my name is Libby Cooper—this bag of bones is my husband."

Gretchen let Coop lean over, practically doubling over in half to shake Margarita's hand. "Very nice meeting you. Where's your guy?"

Margarita frowned and scanned the beach. "Oh! There he is. Isidor. He's there talking to the short one in Spanish."

"Tell him not to believe a word that guy tells him," Coop said and gave her a wink. "Anything at all Libby or I can do to help make your transition easier, you just let us know. There is this phone list. I assume Christy has—"

Gretchen interrupted. "Yes, we've already been over this. You're going to forget all these names, but once you get the list you can make notes. At least that's what I did."

"Awesome."

Libby and Cooper excused themselves, and that

gave Gretchen an opportunity to ask Margarita about her artwork.

"Well, I do large abstract painting, acrylic on canvas. I am self-taught. However, I've been working under a tutor, and we talk online once a week. I have sold two of my paintings to the mayor's office in Chula Vista, which made me very proud."

"That's fantastic. Do you have pictures on you?"

Margarita took out her cell phone and flipped through several screens before she showed Gretchen a portfolio of some of her canvases.

"These are absolutely stunning. I have an artist you have to meet. Her name is Deirdre Gray, and she also does large acrylic paintings. They aren't abstract, but more modern cubist like a blend of Dali and Rousseau, if there is such a thing."

"That would mean jungle scenes and twisted figures, snakes and tigers and green leaves. Is that what she paints?"

"Well, sort of." Gretchen was at a loss to accurately describe Deirdre's portraits and landscapes. "They are huge, some of them eight or ten feet tall. And they're brightly colored, but you could stand there for several minutes and see so many different things inside. They're like little, tiny paintings within paintings, and I don't know how she does it, but it's almost like she puts a little painting in the middle and then paints around it or makes it part of the overall picture. She's also started to do some ceramic work and crazy quilt patchwork. You know, fabric sculpture?"

"Oh, yes, I love that as well. I don't have a proper machine, but, yes, some of the artwork from Mexico is unbelievably beautiful, with all the folklore and the festive colors. It's amazing how intricate and how creative different fabric textures and stitches come together to create a big piece. I've planned a trip to go to Kentucky to visit museums on quilting."

"Fantastic. We'll have to arrange a field trip, because I've never been. So you just have to meet Deirdre. We're in the process of buying a building and setting it up as a home for a catering business, as well as setting up a wedding center. Of course, Deirdre is going to be featuring a lot of her paintings, but she was going to be inviting several other artists to display their works on a rotating basis. I will certainly make sure she gets your name, because I think these would be gorgeous."

Margarita thanked her with a big smile. "When will you have the grand opening? I'd like to come."

"Well, I'm going to say it'll be at least a year. We've just made the offer or are getting ready to make the offer on the building this week. I think it's going to be a fabulous place, and it's very close to where the SEALs train down at the beach. You know, the course and the rubber boats?"

"Oh, yes, I've been told about those boats. And the little bald spot on the top of their head?"

"Yes. My husband has a bald spot that hasn't quite grown back yet, although he came to BUD/s a little bit older than some of the others. But, yes, they all talk of that, don't they?"

Gretchen had almost forgotten Angie and Rebecca had followed them around. Angie spoke up first. "And how their feet turn green when they take off their shoes."

"We had that as well, and, no matter how hard he scrubbed, that green color stayed with him for at least five days afterwards. My girls thought it was funny too," said Margarita.

Gretchen's cell phone rang, and it was Trace.

"Excuse me. My husband is calling." She stepped away but still within eyesight of her two girls. "I've been wondering what happened to you. I started thinking perhaps Tony got you into some trouble, but then I realized that would never happen," Gretchen whispered to him.

"Oh, if you only knew, Gretchen. He's such a mess and seriously wearing me out. I'm just not sure he's going to be able to do it on his own. He's like a big teenager who can't take care of himself because he was too spoiled by his mother."

"The answer is still no."

"No? No about what?" he asked.

"He's not coming to live with us, Trace. There's just no way in hell I'm going to let that man stay in my house. I don't even want him in San Diego."

"Oh, I get you. No, that won't happen. And I don't think it's what he really wants anyway. We got a buyer for the house, and we signed the contract this afternoon. Tomorrow, I'm going to accompany him to deliver some money to people he owes, and depending on how that goes, I will probably come home Tuesday, I hope. Tomorrow, if I can."

"Oh, that's wonderful news, sweetheart. I have missed you so bad."

"I think we have to be prepared for the fact that Tony has probably done so much damage to his reputation, not to mention his body from lack of exercise and all the things he's put into it, and he just doesn't seem to learn, Gretchen. I mean, sometimes I think he is really honest about wanting to clean his life up, and then—other times—it's like he looks at me like I'm crazy when I remind him of what he promised. I honestly wonder if there's some kind of a cognitive decline—because he just doesn't remember stuff."

"Maybe that was beginning to happen before he got in all that trouble. The coaches were pretty upset with him, and I know he felt the pressure."

"I don't know, but I'm doing what I can. The house got sold to a young contractor and his wife, really nice couple. They come from money, so it's an all-cash offer, and they want to close it quickly, so I think the timing's good on all that. I can't stay here too long, because we have the workup, and I got a call from Kyle, and I guess we're going to be deploying sooner than anticipated."

"Oh, pooh. And here I was hoping I'd have you for a month or two."

"Well, don't worry about it. It hasn't happened yet, but I want you to be ready for it."

"I will. I've got two little ladies who are dying to talk to you, Trace. They're standing right next to me."

She handed the phone to Angie first and continued talking about the wedding center space with Margarita while overhearing the conversation. Trace was having fun joking with their daughter. When Rebecca got on the phone, she mentioned to him that they had invited Margarita's children to come over to one of the clinics that she coached for younger kids. Gretchen knew it probably made Trace smile from ear to ear.

Angie grabbed the phone again and asked him, "Daddy, I just wonder if we would be able to have chickens?"

Gretchen stopped mid-sentence, did a double take, and stared at her youngest daughter. "Angie?"

"Well, my friend Cecilia from school, they have a little farm. She has a donkey. And they have chickens. Oh, they're so cute, and I got to hold them, and the mother chicken—guess what? She lays blue eggs."

Gretchen smiled as she listened to Angie, always the most expressive of her three, go into great detail about how the chickens were cared for. Margarita looked on with a big smile on her face too.

"She's really sweet, isn't she?"

"She's always been my live wire. This one here"— she put her arm around Rebecca—"is my athlete. I think if she sticks with it, she could play professional volleyball. She's that good."

Rebecca adopted a reddened, bashful face.

"Do you play, Gretchen?"

"Oh, I bump with the girls from time to time, but mostly, I just shank it, and they have to go chasing after the ball. I'm not all that athletic, but the girls have really enjoyed it, and it's wonderful conditioning."

"I'll make sure the girls watch a practice or two. What does a short girl do on a team? Yours are so tall!"

"The back row position, libero, usually is a short girl who's extremely athletic. Oftentimes, on the good teams, they have someone put in there who has actually done quite a bit of gymnastics, since they literally have to dive for the ball and often do somersaults trying to pass it to their teammates. It's a tough position to play, I think maybe the hardest."

"Really? So a shorter player would still, if she's athletic enough, be able to compete?"

"Well, if she can jump, like high jump type quality, then she can block in the front row. That's where they put the giraffes usually. I call them giraffes because they're all so tall, and they look clumsy as heck when they're teenagers trying to get down and dig a ball. But the little girls in the back row, as long as they get to the ball and can successfully pass, there's a spot for that kind of a player, and she can get things that the tall ones sometimes struggle with."

"I didn't realize."

"In fact, when Clover was playing, their team was huge. I mean, there were thirteen- and fourteen-year-old girls who were over six feet tall on her team. And if you looked at the parents, well, it was a conclave of the giants, if you know what I mean. Well, they played a team from Hawaii, and those girls, I don't think any of them were over five feet tall. Those girls never let a ball hit the floor. They would dive, they would do pancake saves, and they would do cartwheels. Oh my gosh, they were so athletic, and they never let the ball hit the ground. You can be serving balls and spiking them all you want on the one side, but, if the other side returns those balls every time, you don't have to jump and hit it really hard. You just have to not make a mistake, and they beat our girls handily in straight sets. So I have a whole new respect for short volleyball players."

Angie handed the phone back to her mom, probably at Trace's prompting. Gretchen stepped away again and signed off to Trace. "I'm glad you're helping him. Thank you."

"You're welcome. I didn't do it for him, you know that. But I just couldn't live with myself. Leave him out there dangling. Tony doesn't really need a best friend; we need to get him a wife. We need to get him a wife quick. Do you know any prospects?"

"I'm just thinking through the list of our friends who I hate enough to recommend."

All of a sudden, Gretchen had an idea. "I've got the perfect woman for Tony."

"Yeah?"

Gretchen saw an odd couple sneaking off into the shadows.

"I can't wait for it. The suspense is killing me."

She grinned. "Shayla. Your ex!"

CHAPTER 9

T RACE GOT UP early, giving Tony a few extra minutes to rest. It had been a long couple of days, mostly due to the stress of Tony's situation, and it was beginning to take its toll on Trace. He could do action and danger and jumping out of airplanes at thirteen thousand feet at midnight. But this emotional stuff, not knowing who was in charge, who the real enemy was, caused his brain to be on alert twenty-four seven. There were so many aspects to Tony's complicated situation, and some were increasingly becoming more dangerous by the minute.

He straightened the kitchen and picked up Tony's shoes and other things he'd left strewn around the dining room table, made himself some coffee, and called it good. The rest of the place was going to have to wait until the tenants returned.

He took his cell phone and his coffee out on the porch to look over the Columbia River and just collect his thoughts. Often it was the best way to organize all the little loose ends and details going on about a mission, just like he did when he was working an op for SEAL Team 3.

It was beautiful here, cool at nights, unlike San Diego, and he remembered visiting Gretchen, meeting the girls, and falling in love with her in this house. He was a bit sad that it was going to be leaving the family, but it had been so overridden by these terrible tenants, it almost didn't even look like the same property. It was time to move on, he knew. After he married Gretchen, she and the girls were much happier down south with him.

He thought about all the things that could go wrong, not to depress himself, but just so he was mentally prepared if one of those scenarios happened to show its ugly face. He didn't really know much about Sam and The Organization, but he didn't really want to deploy any Navy assets to dig into it, and so the only other person he could talk to would be perhaps Kelly Fielding, who was living in Portland and working on her father-in-law's security company with her sister-in-law, Jenna Riley.

He thought about what he was going to ask her. He wondered what had ever happened to Sven, the Norwegian special ops soldier, highly decorated, they'd used on several missions in Africa, most notably the

Canaries, which was where they were supposed to be going next. He hated that place. Last Trace had heard, Sven and Kelly were an item and made a good team.

Tony had turned out to be more of a handful than he'd calculated. He doubted even Gretchen knew how far out of control he was. He was cocky, argumentative, and more like an ill-mannered teenager with too much money and not enough common sense. He knew he wasn't going to be able to control him as much as he needed, and—especially during his deployment—it might be a dangerous time for Tony. If there was any way they could put this whole thing to bed before Trace left the country, that would be ideal.

Part of him regretted ever volunteering for the mission. But he also understood that evil had a way of breaking out just when you thought it was contained, and, when that happened, all bets were off. Bad news could just streak across anybody's life, embroil many more innocent people, like Gretchen and the girls, and would continue getting bigger and bigger until someone stomped it out with force. So it was better that he was involved, even though he just wasn't sure how this whole thing was going to end.

He dialed Kelly's number, and she picked it up on the first ring.

"Oh my God, Trace Bennett. It's been—what?—a year, two maybe since we talked last?"

Trace had thought for sure he would wake her up, but she was chipper and ready to work. She must have been using her spin cycle or went for an early workout.

"Yes, ma'am. None other."

"Does this mean you're in Portland?"

"I am. I'm up here with Gretchen's ex, Tony."

"The basketball player?"

"The same."

"I didn't think you two were friends at all. So what gives? You still sticking with Kyle and the team, or are you about ready to jump ship and come work for us?"

Trace chuckled. "Nah, I'd make too many demands on you, Kelly. The first thing you'd have to do is move your whole operation to Coronado because there's no way in hell I'm going to live in Portland."

"I get it. I wish he hadn't set it up here either, and we're looking. But I'm not sure San Diego would be our first choice. But definitely not the Pacific Northwest."

He heard sounds of a male voice in the background so Trace didn't want to intrude. "I see you've got company, Kelly. Can I call you back later?"

He heard the distinct voice of Sven Tolar growling behind her. "Kelly, what the hell?"

"You want to talk to him, Trace? Warning you. He's in a foul mood."

"Yeah, I'll talk to him."

Kelly and Sven had a battle over the cell phone, and Sven won.

"How are you, Trace? You're here in Portland?"

"Yep. I came into town on Friday. I'm with Gretchen's ex, Tony. He got released from prison, and he's got himself in a little bit of trouble, so I've picked him up and am helping him raise some money so he can get rid of that trouble."

"Don't you give him any money. From what I've been told, the guy's a loser. He's not long for this world, Trace. You need to go back home. But not before you see us, okay?"

"Well, partly the reason I called is to see if you or Kelly had any information about the group that's kind of got him by the cojones. It is called The Organization. Have you heard of them?"

"Oh yeah. Can I put this on speakerphone?"

"Are we secure?"

"We're not wired, and I sweep regularly, and it's just the two of us in the house now. So yeah, I'd say so."

"Knock yourself out then."

"So how did he get mixed up with The Organization? These are really bad dudes."

"Oh, I know. I've only met one of them, and I could see right away that they have something in common with Tony."

"What's that? Or is this a joke?"

"They're stupid, and they're dangerous. And that combination of the two makes them even more dangerous. I'm up here just because it's a favor to Gretchen and the girls. If I can't get him straight with this guy, not sure what to do. Wish I could just cut him loose. Even if I wanted to, I can't give him any money. I mean, we're hand to mouth as it is with two in college. Just finished paying the last check for Clover's wedding."

"Clover got married?" Kelly asked.

"Yeah, married a really nice kid who's studying to be a veterinarian, but he's kind of excited about all the SEALs he saw at his wedding. Oh gosh, he's asked me to train him. But don't you say a word, because Clover doesn't know yet."

"Ouch," said Sven. "That's a huge mistake. I hope you set him right."

"I did. I *think* he heard me."

"Geez, did you bring Gretchen and the other two with you?"

"Nah, Tony was in the facility just outside of Eugene, and it's really too dangerous for her and the girls to be involved in any of this. I want to keep them out as long as I can. We met with a guy who I guess is the money man. He gave us instructions. We're on our way to give a little down payment, and then Tony's going to give him the rest of the cash after his house sells."

"Here in Portland?" Kelly asked.

"Yeah, it's the one Gretchen used to live in. I think you've been here a couple times, guys."

"Oh, I know it now. Nice view of the river?" she added.

"That's it. Anyway, he's had it rented out while he was in the can, and we already got a buyer for it, a young contractor and his wife. They're going to pay all cash, take it 'as is,' and close it quickly, which is good news for us. Before he hands over all that money, I wanted to see if I could get more information about these people. I mean, they might take the money and then murder us both or set it up so that we get compromised somehow, and that's all she wrote, end of story, right?"

"No, you don't want to do that. Yeah, you need to find out who's really running the show. You need some help?"

"I just need information."

"I'll tell you what. You buy us breakfast, and we will meet away from downtown. I've got a favorite little diner called Betty's Butter Biscuits down in the warehouse district."

"Yes, I know it well. Tyler's mom and dad had that gallery that burned down. I was going to stop by and pay my respects."

"They moved down there, didn't they?" asked Sven.

"Yes, I meant, pay my respects to all the beautiful paintings that Deirdre lost in the fire. Just about broke her. But she's doing really well, and they've got a big project they're working on. I'll let them tell you sometime when we get together."

"Cool. Well, I'm hungry. I don't know about you," Sven said. "So we'll meet you down at Betty's in say thirty, forty-five minutes? Does that work?"

"If I can get Prince Charming up. He's been snoring up a storm, so I think he slept pretty good, but I sure didn't."

"Tell me you didn't sleep in the same bed with the asshole."

"No, sir. I would've slept on the floor. I would've slept in the garage, but I was not going to sleep in the same bed as Tony. Not to worry, Sven. And quit mothering me, for Christ's sake. I've got a wife and three daughters who do a lot of that. So just stop it, okay?"

"I get you. You want to go check on lover boy and let us know if it's a no-go?"

From behind Trace, Tony yelled out, "No, I'm awake. We'll be there. Thirty minutes max."

Trace turned around to see Tony dressed in a woman's pair of pajamas, the fabric colored in bright pink and yellow pigs, surrounded by daffodils and angels. He looked ridiculous in the outfit. However, he knew Tony didn't own a pair of pajamas because he only owned three pieces of clothing, and Trace had seen them all.

"Well, we'll see you down there then. It looks like we're a go," said Trace. He hung up the phone. Turning to Tony, he asked, "Goddamn it, Tony, what the hell's going on now? Are we adding cross-dressing to your list of transgressions?"

"It's the only thing she had that had long sleeves. It was dark. I couldn't see and I was cold, man."

"What'd you wear in the joint?"

"As many pieces of clothing as I could: sweatshirt, sweatpants, socks. I covered up, man. I was cold all the time. I tossed all that shit before I left. Didn't need the memories. I think the heat's turned off here. I was freezing."

"Well, let's get you fixed up. You like the coffee?"

Tony held his mug up. "Yeah, it's just the way I like it."

"I was going to apologize that we didn't have any half-and-half, but I was afraid to leave you alone. Wasn't sure you'd be here when I got back."

"Come on, Trace. You've got to understand I'm in this for the long haul. I'm trying to get my life turned around, and I'm not going to bail on this whole thing and become a fugitive. I got too much going for me."

Trace silently disagreed with Tony, but he didn't want to waste the energy trying to argue with him. "You just get your butt in the shower. I'll follow, and we'll get down there and talk to my friend."

As Trace pushed Tony through the living room and out to the back bathroom, he was peppered with questions from the former NBA star.

"Sven has a history of European Special Forces, and we've used him on ops before, outside of the U.S. He's now working with his fiancée, I think. I'm not sure they got married, but she helps run a security firm that she and her sister-in-law inherited, and they do all kinds of special projects for major players in business and political. And, on occasion, Uncle Sam has been known to task them with a few things. That's how we initially met them. Kelly has a background in State Department work. She was married to the owner's son, who died from a drug overdose."

"Nice people, huh?

"No, they are. Other than my SEAL buddies, I wouldn't want anybody else to have my back but those two. Someday, I might go to work for them. But, for right now, I'm going to ask them a favor."

"What kind of a favor?" Tony asked.

"I'll tell you at breakfast. Now get your butt in the shower and let's leave this place in about ten minutes max, okay?"

"You've got it."

Betty's Butter Biscuits looked like a hopping place at 7:30 in the morning, with a line of customers about twenty deep extending from the front door halfway down to the corner. The patrons appeared to be an eclectic group, some professional people in suits and others, students, dressed casual for school. It was a testament to how good Betty's biscuits must be, thought Trace.

"Was this here when you were with Gretchen?" he asked. "I don't remember seeing it before."

"No, I think it's new."

Trace looked for a parking spot and, after driving around the block twice, finally managed to snag one from a customer just leaving.

They didn't see Kelly and Sven in the line of people waiting, so Trace led the way and checked out the tiny dining room.

"Ah, there they are," he said. The two were sitting in a far corner, nice and private, just like Trace liked it. When he and Sven made eye contact, Sven got up, crossed the room in three oversized strides, and gave him a big hug.

"It's been way too long, son. God, you're getting old."

"Let's keep it honest, Sven. You're not more than a

couple of months older than I am," Trace answered.

Kelly waved and remained seated at the table, sipping her coffee. Sven snagged the waitress and ordered a couple more coffees for Trace and Tony. "If that's all right?"

"And I'll have cream if you have it," said Trace.

Trace began his introductions.

"So this is Tony, Gretchen's ex. I don't think you guys have met yet, right?"

"No, I would've remembered it. Nice to meet you, Tony." They shook hands, and then Sven introduced him to Kelly Fielding. "Have a seat, guys," he said to the two of them.

The waitress brought their coffees, and Sven indicated they had already ordered so Tony and Trace added theirs.

"So what's going on?" asked Sven.

"I overheard part of your conversation, Mr. Tolar. I don't appreciate your opinion of me. But, just for the record, we just want some background information on this group, The Organization?" Tony's voice was laced with lots of attitude, and Trace noted that Sven picked up on it right away.

"Uh-huh. Now, son, there's a rule about dealing with people like that."

"You mean don't do it, right? Fuck, I know that already. You don't have to tell me that."

"Well, first of all, you don't go announcing it to a room full of strangers, okay?"

Tony turned in his seat and studied the customers eating all around him.

"So if you're going to talk about these people, I want you to be quiet about it. It's just not smart."

"God, you guys are all so touchy."

Kelly inserted her opinion, "That's how they stay alive, Tony. You could learn a lot from these two."

"Okay, so I get it. Let me say it over again then. We just want information. I mean, I think Trace has a point. We want to make sure—if we work out a deal with them—that they'll honor their side."

Sven pushed his chair back from the table, nearly tipping over, and laughed. "Oh, you're concerned they won't honor the deal? That's exactly what they do, Tony. They keep changing it on you all the time. They'll say, 'Oh, you got to do this' and then 'Oh, you got to do this' and then pretty soon you're in it so deep you'll never get out. As a matter of fact, we could sit here and talk ten years from now, and you'd still be stuck with them. And you would've paid them a lot of money."

"Well, I think they underestimated me."

Trace looked over at him carefully, and then he gave a blank expression to Sven before he answered, "Honestly, Tony, every time I think you say something stupid, you say something even more stupid. They're working with you because they think you're their bitch, Tony. They're going to milk you until you're dead," he whispered between his teeth.

Sven jumped in. "The only way we have a shot at it is if we negotiate, get them paid off, and perhaps make it not worth their while to hassle you anymore."

Trace wondered how in the hell that could happen. Their choices were limited.

Sven inquired further. "Tell me again who you're dealing with. Are they all local guys, or are you talking to people from out of the country?"

The waitress interrupted them by presenting their breakfast, which looked fabulous. Trace was going to have to restrain himself not to order double and triple orders of biscuits.

"I always did kind of like gambling a little bit, and I did some work for them. There was a group in L.A. I got involved with, to help them set up their online gambling platform and, you know, help them promote. Their thing was run from someplace offshore but, as long as I wasn't betting on my teams or anything professional in the U.S., I could still promote it. Or at least that's what they said. Anyway, it turned out that wasn't true either. When the team found out, I had to cancel on the deal or nullify my player contract, and, of course, that incurred fees."

"Of course," Sven said.

"And then, after things started unraveling with my coach and the team, I was kind of stupid. You know Gretchen and I split up. I just kind of went on a little bit of a spiral, and we had that altercation between me and Trace, and … Anyway, I got four years, and I was doing pretty good with that. In fact, I was even doing some gambling from the facility here in Eugene, and then things started to go sour. I got in a couple fights, and then I started losing bets. And then, what do you know? All of a sudden, I'm doing nine and a quarter years. Just hardly doesn't even seem fair. I was the victim here."

Trace noted Sven's glazed-over look. Tony was not making points with him.

"So then what happened? How did you pay them? They kill people who don't."

"Well, before long I was in it so hard that, you know, they had carried me. The interest was bigger than the original money they lent to me, so I'm stuck, and I got to sell the house, which we did, by the way. We've done a lot of work, haven't we, Trace?"

Trace nodded his head in full agreement.

"Anyway, I'm to give him $50,000 today. I got an equity line on the house, and then I'm supposed to pay him the rest later. In about two weeks, the escrow will close, and, after commissions and everything, I think they'll get about seven maybe. I'd like to have a little to live on, but he doesn't seem to be very interested in that."

"And who is *he*?"

"Sam, the guy I'm dealing with in Eugene."

"Okay, so it's his money that bankrolled you?"

"Yes, at least he's the one who owns the guys in the facility I was in. They all work for him, doing various things. I figured I was going to get back on the court, Sven, and it even looked like they had a shot for me at one of the G leagues, and there was going to be a signing bonus that was going to be good for me. I had retirement saved up, a little bit left over from my contract. But the rest of it they voided when I went to prison. And then it got spent on attorney's fees, as their guys tried to negotiate this deal."

"Don't tell me. They scared them off, right?"

Tony nodded. "In the end, it all fell through, and then I started losing, and the debts really started piling up. So I'm kind of in a pickle. I'm worried they'll come after me if I don't give them the money."

"So how much money are you going to be short after you sell the house?" asked Sven.

"I think about one fifty, maybe two? It's kind of hard getting specific numbers. He charges what he wants to charge as far as interest, like twenty percent a month, and, um, you know, he just more or less tells me whatever he wants to tell me, so it's hard to follow the plan."

Sven had been shaking his head during the last part of Tony's pathetic statement. His expression was pained.

"Of course, it's designed that way, Tony. You do know that they're not going to let you go, right?"

"Well, what about the thing you said. That we make it inconvenient or difficult for them to do business with us. Isn't that what you said?"

"Yeah, something like that. But you don't want to be dealing with these people long-term. You want to try to get out of it with the first offer and then walk away. I mean, I don't ever want you guys … I think it would be stupid of you to have anything further to do with them. You understand that, don't you?"

"Hell, yeah."

"So let me tell you a little bit about this 'Organization.' You may not know, but they also are involved in other things, prostitution, some drugs, and extortion. But their real specialty is providing young girls for businessmen, household slaves, sex slaves, and they get their girls from foreign countries that are embroiled in skirmishes. War is good for business."

"But nobody ever said anything about—"

Both Trace and Sven whispered tersely, "Quiet!"

Sven finished his coffee and sighed. "They're captured, sold to these guys, and these guys ... I mean, it's just like a farmers market, right? They pick them up, clean them up, and sell them to the highest bidder. That's where they make the real money, and they hook some of their business clients, people like yourself with big incomes or used to have big incomes, to help them. Or to turn them on to their friends. Once they get their hooks in one person in the group, then they go after the whole group to try to be an indispensable addition."

"That's just pure evil."

"So is gambling, drinking to excess, many of those very same vices I believe you have, Tony. They're very dangerous. They're ruthless, and they are so good they're even working through some of this country's legitimate NGOs, so our Uncle Sam tax dollars fund some of their projects. Everybody loves to save children, right? Refugee children especially, and there's a whole lot of them being brought into this country right now. It's lucrative, and I don't think our government has the will or the brains to solve it. And there is an unlimited source of young children being orphaned by all the wars all over this planet. War pays. It also kills. But it pays well."

"So, Sven, how do we stop this?" Tony asked.

"I'll tell you what ... I'm going to go with you and Trace today to deliver the first payment. We'll discuss the terms for the balance. I want to meet your guy. I want to see what he's about, and I'm going to make him an offer."

Trace immediately interrupted. "Sven, I didn't ask you to do this," he objected. "I didn't ask for you to bail him out. Don't do that. It's a losing proposition."

"It's just one poker hand, Trace. We do this one thing, and we lose the round, but we win the game that way. I have to get them off his back, and then we go back, and we create a little mayhem. Not so as anybody would notice, but just a little payback. And who knows? I might get my money back." He smiled.

Trace looked back and forth between Kelly and Sven. "You would do that for Tony?"

"No, Trace. I do that for you. Because you care most about the people they're going to ruin if we don't make this deal. Our job is to keep them away from Gretchen and the girls. Trust me when I tell you this, Trace, the only way you can have a prayer of getting them off his back is to pay them. Pay them whatever they want. And they'll go away for a while. That's when we play our second hand."

"And what's our second hand?" Tony eagerly asked.

Sven crossed his arms and glanced down at Kelly, who smiled back, and it was obvious to Trace that they'd discussed the whole thing. He knew the answer

Sven was going to give them even before he said it.

"I haven't quite figured that out yet. But when I do, Tony, you're going to be a standup guy, and you're going to be right in the middle of it."

They finished breakfast, agreeing to meet back at Tony's house. Trace and Tony packed up what they had, including the cash Tony picked up on the way home. They left a note for the tenants that they'd need a couple extra days. When Sven arrived, they took Trace's rental to Eugene to meet with Sam.

"He's very pushy, Sven. So don't get pissed off if he disses you," Tony cautioned.

Trace cursed quietly as he drove on. He saw Sven smiling at him in the rearview mirror.

"No need to give me the particulars. I'm going to be checking out other things. Not to worry. This time, he gets a free pass and can say whatever he wants. Next time will be different."

The bar and grill looked the same as it did before. The light dusting of rain felt dirty on Trace's face and neck, but—when he entered the place—he felt the thick smoke of cigars and dope plaster to his wet face like a facial mask. It added to his irritation, but he quickly adjusted his mental state to stay alert to something he wouldn't expect.

Sam was already sitting at the table with his whiskey. This time he didn't offer any to Trace and Tony.

His dark, squinting eyes bored into Sven.

"Who's this jerk?" he asked.

"Extra protection," Trace said before Tony could stumble through a word salad.

"Are you packing?" Sam asked him.

"Fucking A, I am," answered Sven.

Trace felt the tension in the air. Sam was considering his options.

"Anytime I carry more than a grand, I'm armed, and you would be too. So let's move on and get this thing handled," Sven continued.

"You a foreigner?" Sam asked.

"None of your business. Russian, if you must know."

Trace almost split a gut. Tony started to object, and Trace stepped on his big toe. Hard.

"So let's see the money."

"Let's drink first," Sven said, startling everyone.

No one moved. Even the bartender was waiting for instructions from Sam.

"You heard the man. Bring the bottle and some glasses, or are you a vodka drinker?"

"I prefer whiskey in this part of the country. The vodka you'd serve me would be horse pee," answered Sven.

The bartender started across the room with the three glasses rattling and a bottle, setting them down on the table, and was back behind the bar in a flash.

Sven poured the glasses, added some to Sam's and then they held their drinks in the air.

"To enemies becoming friends long enough to make some money. To ending conflict, with everyone walking away alive."

It was an odd toast, but Trace nodded and drank, as did Tony.

"Another!" Sven insisted.

Trace shook his head when the bottle was presented to him, but Sven argued with him. "It's required. Otherwise, you're out of this deal completely."

Trace knew it was a masking type of maneuver, showing a lack of respect, a little wrinkle or crack in their wall of defense, showing it on purpose. He was tempted to just agree and walk out. He wanted nothing more of this situation, but he went along anyway.

"Of course, if it's required, I'll do it."

They all toasted again, this time with Sam's callout. "To the gamble of life. To burying enemies both foreign and domestic."

Trace was now grateful for the platter of ham, eggs and all the biscuits he consumed, as it was a good antidote to the alcohol. He had a few hours of driving to do, up to Portland again then back to Eugene and a possible flight out. All of this were the steps he had to take to get free.

"So you are Sam, no?" Sven asked.

"I am, and you may sit at my table now."

All three of them did so. Trace noted the room was nearly empty. Of the patrons who were there, none looked like part of Sam's gang or henchmen, but he guessed there could be some upstairs watching on a TV monitor remotely.

"How much does this asshole owe you?"

"Nine fifty, plus." Sam grinned, and Trace noted he had a gold tooth in front.

"Nine fifty. No plus. All interest stops for thirty days."

"No, sir, Tony knows and has already agreed to pay twenty percent a month on top of the principal."

"Except some of the principle is made up of carried interest, so it isn't principle at all. You're making profit on profit."

"What's it to you?"

"I'm looking out for you, Sam. Because if you don't accept the nine fifty in thirty days or less, then the next offer is going to be eight fifty. Then seven fifty … and so on. This is your best deal."

"You can't do that."

"I just did. So are you turning down the offer of nine fifty? You get all of it in thirty days, cash."

"What about today?"

"I'm taking that off the table next."

"Hold on there, asshole. I'm not agreeing to that."

"The kid's gotta live. He's gotta look for a job and get a car. He needs money for that. How much do you need today? Are you that hard up you can't give him a chance to conduct his business to get you the rest of the money?"

"I need fifty."

"I already told you that was going next. Now it's forty."

"I said fifty."

"Okay then, it's thirty. Are you ready to stop?"

"No, man."

"You go down to twenty. But today you're a lucky man, Sam. You get $25,000 today and the rest in thirty days. That's the best you're gonna get, or we go get our other negotiators, and we make some calls to the U.S. Marshall's office and the Eugene District Attorney. Ken Wheeler is his name. I know him on a first name basis. I think he'd want to know about this shake-down—"

"Fuck you. Okay, I'll take it. But you and me, we have a score to settle later."

"Looking forward to that, Sam. Can't wait. I do my best negotiations in a ring, or tarmac, or in a bar, like this one. Of course, there's always collateral damage. But you know that's part of the cost."

"You are a dead man."

"Really?" Sven checked himself out, padding his chest and frowning. "I think you're wrong. I'm very much alive, and, remember, I do have something that will put a four-inch hole in your chest. So play nice, Sam, and you'll be forced to take nearly a million dollars off this pathetic kid who happened to fall in your shithole. But you're gonna keep your hands off him after you get paid. Understood?"

"Just give me the twenty-five."

"You gotta give me your word, in front of all these people here. Otherwise, I let my little friend do the talking."

Several of the patrons left through side doors, unlikely to return, from their expressions. Even the bartender sat down behind the countertop.

"I promise."

"To kill me? Come on, to do what?"

"It's settled after I get the full nine fifty. Tony's hands-off."

"And you tell The Organization too?"

Sam smiled, obviously enjoying his lie. "Yeah, I tell them to keep their hands off too." He started chuckling.

Sven directed Tony to give him the money. He counted out the $25,000 and dropped it in front of Sam in wads tied in bank paper.

"You should be proud. I walked in here prepared to

give you nothing. My Russian friends will think I've gone soft. So don't tell them if they happen to stop by just to check to make sure you didn't leave town."

Sam collected his money and, for a few seconds, looked like a little boy with all the money and houses in a Monopoly game he'd just won.

CHAPTER 10

GRETCHEN AND ANGIE were baking an apple pie when Trace quietly tiptoed through the front door and approached them in the kitchen, both of them covered in flour. Gretchen heard him come up behind her, heard his familiar, raspy breathing as her heart instinctively skipped a couple of beats. She turned just as he grabbed her.

"Trace!" Gretchen collapsed into his arms and was so grateful he had returned she wasn't going to chastise him for not making that phone call to let her know he was back in Coronado.

"Well, mission accomplished?" she couldn't help but ask.

"It's all been sort of worked out for now. As long as Tony gets the house sold, it's game over."

"How the heck did you do that?" she asked him as Angie gave him a careful hug, still depositing flour on his cheek.

Trace glanced between the two of them. "I'll tell you about it later." He paused and then smiled at their youngest. "Angie, how are your games going?"

"Really well, Trace. We've got a dynamite team this year. The new girls are awesome, and I think we could win some titles. I've signed them up for some camps and some festivals where they can play against some great teams from all over the U.S."

"Awesome. Road trips?"

"Yes. We'll be taking those in June and July. It's just amazing what these girls are doing. I wasn't half as good as they are at their age."

"Well, let's see. You're fourteen, and they're twelve?"

"No, Trace, they're eight and nine years old. But they're already nearly six feet tall some of them. I mean, it's amazing. And the parents are so into it. It's really a joy."

"So maybe you have future plans to go into coaching then. I mean, that's a huge career field. It would have a good, solid future."

Gretchen felt her stomach rumbling. She could feel a boundary being breached.

"Trace," she started. "She's having a great time. I don't want her to think that she has to do this for the rest of her life. Let her take the win and enjoy it, no pressure. She's got lots of time to decide what she wants to do. Love you, but sometimes a kid just needs to be a kid. Right?"

Trace nodded his head. "Yes, ma'am. Whatever you say."

With another kiss to both of them, he dashed upstairs to unpack and take a shower.

Angie whispered, "Mom, you're kind of hard on him sometimes. He just was trying to be nice."

"I'm aware of that, sweetheart. I just don't want him to push too hard. You've got your father as an example. I think Clover would still be playing basketball today if he hadn't pushed so forcefully."

"I get your meaning. He did do that a lot. It wasn't pleasant."

"It's just not at all like what it used to be. These sports teams are so competitive. And I get it, it's a good thing to go for, but not at the exclusion of family and just being a teenager, Angie. It doesn't always have to be coaching a winning team or coming in number one. That's what you go for, and, hey, I have no problem with that, but just because you're coaching eight- and ten-year-old girls doesn't mean that's going to be your trajectory. I want you to keep all your options open. And yes, Angie, I'm very, very proud of you. But you know that!"

Angie hugged her. "Mom, you're the best. I got lucky in that department, didn't I?"

"Thanks, Angie." Gretchen practically melted. Tears came to her eyes, which she quickly covered.

"I even got lucky with the men in your life."

Gretchen thought to herself that her taste in men had improved greatly since her very first choice of Tony. Now she understood what a real man was, and, now that she'd found him, she was all in. Nothing would ever change her mind.

Gretchen and Angie finished their pie and put it in the oven while Trace followed up with some of his teammates. He got a call from Sven and walked outside to take it. Gretchen suspected Sven had something to do with the outcome of Tony's deal.

There was a gathering later on over at the Brownlee residence, a pool party, and several of the couples were going. Gretchen told Trace about the new men who had joined the team and a couple of the wives that she'd met the day before.

"Your new Mexican recruit's wife, Margarita, and I had a good discussion about art and the project we're working on. She's also a painter. You should see her work."

"You point them out to me and we'll say hello."

Austin Brownlee was in a good mood, flanked by his new girlfriend, Melissa Murphy, and flatly put down rumors that they'd gotten engaged, but they were living together and, for all intents and purposes, were married in every way but one.

Gretchen, at first, had been resistant to the relationship, mostly because of the initial drama of their appearance in Coronado. Austin's twin brother, Will Brownlee, had been a SEAL killed in Grenada. Years later, Melissa and her daughter, Will Brownlee's child, had shown up on Austin's doorstep to get to know the family. Austin's wife had passed away over a year now, and the two were accepted into the extended family after everything came out. Knowing all the details now, it seemed like Austin and Melissa's attraction and love story were written in the stars.

She reminded herself that none of them ever knew what the future held for them. Things could change on a dime. Idea was, Trace told her, that they all keep on living, enjoying the freedoms the SEALs and many others they worked with protected for them.

"Best way to honor them is to live your life fully," he'd told her.

That wise advice had worked miracles in her life. Once, she'd thought her life was a mess and doubted any romance would ever come her way. Now she was certain the love she and Trace held for each other was borne out of the hardships of loss, feeling forgotten, and being alone. All that had changed. She feared not having him by her side.

The two of them made the rounds. Near the lounge

chairs, Angie stripped off her clothes down to her bathing suit and talked to several of the other SEAL kids, who frolicked in the pool until a couple of the Team Guys came in and took over. They splashed and created such a stir the girls got out, yet the boys tried to compete.

On the way home, Gretchen told him how the project was coming.

"You gonna take me by to see it?"

She turned to Angie in the second seat. "You mind?"

"No, I'm fine. I'd like to see it too."

She directed the way to the warehouse just south of the base, and they got out to walk around the building. They couldn't see much of the inside due to the fact that the windows were taped over in some places and, in other places, just plain dirty. It looked like someone was in the process of painting it.

"So you got this building? All signed, sealed, delivered?" he asked.

"No, I don't think so. I am concerned about this paint though. This wasn't here a couple of days ago. But we're negotiating, I guess. I'm leaving all of that up to Deirdre and Kate. And they weren't at the party today, so I wonder what the heck's going on with that." Gretchen allowed the wave of concern to brush over her.

"Well, maybe they had it scheduled before the offer went through. Maybe the owners wanted to make it look more attractive to draw more interest."

They walked the grounds, and Gretchen pointed out the fact that from the second story you could see the ocean.

"Nice! That will be a winner!"

"The other thing we like, including the view up-stairs, is the plan Deirdre drew up that calls for a big platform on top overlooking the center and the first floor down below, so it would be a place to sit or have tables for a small, quiet get-together during a larger party. It's also right across the street from where you guys used to train, if you remember?"

"How could I forget?"

"And around the back, we have lots of room for catering trucks and extra storage if we need to bring it in. I mean, Trace, you would just not believe the drawings I've seen, and it just looks like a perfect complex. It's a cooking school, a wedding or party venue, and an art gallery all rolled up into one. I'm excited they even want me to be a part of it since I can't contribute anything."

"You contributed a lot, Gretchen. I think it'd be really thrilling, and look at all the fun Angie would have working down here, don't you agree?" He looked at Angie.

"I told Mom I'd love to learn how to do catering, and it looks like she's going to start a school or something. I know I have several girlfriends who would take her up on the offer to be an apprentice. It's just something I never thought I'd be doing, but I love to cook just like Mom does. With all the parties and things that Mom and Aunt Kate could throw together, I think it's ideal for them. And I think the people would come."

"I'm proud of you, Gretchen. I really can see the vision here. You think big," he said as he bent down and kissed her.

"They are the inspiration. Honest. I'm just one of the team members."

Later on that evening, she sat with Trace and was filled in with further details about what went on in Portland.

"How was it seeing Sven and Kelly?"

"They're considering moving their operation. And, of course, they asked me to join them again. I didn't say anything or let them know that we talked."

She and Trace had talked about the someday when he might want to do something else other than be on the teams. He'd put in his six years, and that was good enough. He would be up for re-enlistment soon, and that was the time when they had to make a decision. They could use the bonus money, Gretchen thought to herself, as they were not exactly flush with cash, but it would mean that he'd have to re-up for another four or six and that would place him near fifty years old when he got out. She didn't think that was a good idea.

"So if you want to consider it, I'm okay with you discussing it with them, real numbers and figures. You know, I kind of think Tyler's in the same boat, and there're several others too. Being on the teams is kind of a young man's deal. What do you think?"

"Well, it would give me flexibility, as long as we can limit the days away and the danger. But I really don't want to live in Portland. I wish they'd moved down here. I'd like to find out what they're thinking first. But, you know, it's a possibility, Gretchen. I could see us staying here—"

"Oh, of course, I love it here, Trace. I don't want to move again."

"That's what I'm saying. We could stay here, and, you know, if I have to travel a little bit, well, that's okay. But I just don't want to spend more time than I have to up in the Pacific Northwest. It's cold and just not my place. Too much negative history there. If all that hadn't happened, I might feel differently. It is a beautiful area, but it's not for me. And you've found a place here, with people you love, and that will continue whether or not I'm still on the teams. I'd consider other places, but I think they'd be better off to be down here. This is where a lot of the tactical companies are, equipment manufacturers, and training centers. They'd have a steady stream of SEALs getting out of the business and looking for something to do, investing in things down here. I think it's a wise decision if they chose that. But we'll see."

"What are they doing these days?"

"Well, I guess they're doing some things in Europe and in Africa, but, with their success with the trafficking, I think they're gonna focus on the women and children being kidnapped and sold. And I talked to Sven a little bit about why he was so interested in helping Tony. It appears that this group that Tony got hooked up with is actually a major player in human trafficking, especially children and girls."

"Did he know that when he got involved?" asked Gretchen.

"No, I don't think he did. I just think he succumbed to his demons, and that led him down the wrong path. I don't think any of us realized how deep their roots went. They're all over the world, Gretchen, even in Europe and Africa."

"Geez, that's horrible. So you think Sven is interested in going after these folks after the fact?"

"I do. I think he's hoping he can find and target some of these people, get some financial help from those who want to also join the cause, and he could find more than enough work. I'm not sure working for the government is going to hold out very much longer. It's a little too dicey for everybody, and you don't have the protections we used to have when we did things. But for private foundations, like the one that they inherited, that's the way to go. They'll keep it legal, but they'll help remove that scourge."

"A worthy goal."

"Besides, the innocent public needs someone standing up for them, someone who can help train them to think like a warrior, teach them how to keep themselves and their families safe. The government is too busy putting out fires elsewhere."

Gretchen saw that his face was animated, his eyes twinkled, as the idea seemed to appeal to him. She made a note to make sure she asked all her questions, because it looked like her man was going to make some changes, and she just wanted him to be safe. It wasn't enough to just have money to live on; she wanted him to be safe.

As they made love that evening, she let the worries drift off and allowed herself to feel the power and love of an ordinary man who did extraordinary things. Someone who loved as hard as he worked. Who would always be there for her, no matter what.

It was an honor to bring to their bed all the passion she found deep down in her soul. He deserved this, and so did she. They were both lucky to have each other.

CHAPTER 11

T RACE PICKED UP Tyler on their way to a full workout at Gunny's gym. They tossed the irons around and spotted for each other, making cracks at some of the older SEALs who liked to frequent the gym early in the morning, and Trace was introduced to a couple of the newbies who were just starting their SEAL Team 3 journey.

"You know the thing that I love about coming here is I can see myself in twenty or thirty years. Like these guys," Trace said, pointing to several grey-haired, beefy men covered in tats who were laughing and enjoying themselves and their self-punishment. They grunted and groaned loudly.

Tyler nodded. "I don't know that I want to look like all of them but, yeah, some of them are in pretty good shape."

Trace laid down to work on a thigh extension machine. He asked Tyler to up the weight a bit and then began his reps.

"You know, nothing wrong with a white ponytail, little bit of a paunch, and muscles like that—look at those guys' muscles and their thighs. I mean, they don't look like the kind of guys who you would want to mess with, right?"

"Yeah, you're right. Certainly would make the women and children feel better walking around with old guys like that."

"I think of the way my grandfather looked in his seventies and eighties. Some of the older men in my family were strong because they worked for a living their whole lives, on farms and machinery and heavy labor work, but they didn't look anything like that. And I'm not saying I want to be a bodybuilder or anything."

He stopped the repetitions enough to take his breath and rest up for the next rep.

"I get what you mean. The ones we don't see in here, of course, are the ones who got injured. And there are some of those in wheelchairs or walkers or who can't stand up straight. Can't hear, can't see, can't sleep through the night from pain. Bad knees, hips, heart."

"Yeah. And that's too bad, isn't it, Tyler? I mean, they gave so much, and they get so little recognition for it."

"Hey, is this *you* talking?" Tyler asked. "When did you expect to get a bunch of medals or recognition for any of the shit you did? You know what it's like, Trace. We do what we do; then we fade back into the woodwork. We're not supposed to be drawing attention to ourselves. If you want to do that, well, go into politics or, I don't know, start a corporation or do a bunch of TED Talks. Write a book, a tell-all book about SEALs."

"Nah, not my style, but some who do, I respect it, if it's good work. Not trash talking. I don't think I have anything that I want anybody to follow me on. I mean, I just want to get my job done, make sure nobody around me gets killed, protect the family, and have a good life."

"You do have a good life, Trace. You found what you needed all along. Some of us get there right away, and some of us have to wait about twenty years or so before we get it. But once you get it, you get it. I once heard of a grandfather of a SEAL who got married again at eighty years old. Can you believe it?"

"Good for them. That's the way it should be, shouldn't it? We never stop falling in love, do we?"

Tyler leaned in and whispered in his ear. "Shh. You don't want anyone to know that. We're big, tough guys, but, inside, we're really softies, right?"

As Trace started another repetition, he boomed out, "Fucking A!"

The comment made the room turn around and take notice. Tyler gave him a wink and shot him with his finger gun. "Now that's what I'm talking about."

After their workout, they went for a run on the beach, passing groups of team guys practicing certain maneuvers, playing football, running in and out of the surf, or lying down and getting wet and sandy voluntarily.

As they ran past, both Tyler and Trace laughed at the ridiculousness of people even trying to do wet and sandies when they didn't have to.

"That would never be me. I don't want to see another rubber boat unless I have to use it for a training exercise or a rescue. No more rubber boats for me. Gretchen asked me if I should get a little Zodiac. We could go out fishing, and I said, hell, no. If I get a boat, it's going to be a big old fucking fishing boat. And then we can go out and anchor and spend all night making that thing rock and roll."

"Well, at least I can report back to my wife that her sister is being well taken care of," said Tyler, with laughter, barely able to get it out.

"Damn straight. No, Gretchen is one of those women who never thought she could get much, and, when you shower her with everything you've got, she just melts and blooms into some fantastic goddess. It's just amazing to see. I feel an ache in my heart at what she missed for so many years, but I'm also very proud of the fact that she's loving life now and that she sees more to the future than she thinks about the past. And that's a good thing, right?"

"That's right. That's the way it should be. So, speaking of futures," Tyler said as he stopped and they both breathed heavy to recover. "You think about what's the next on the road for you?"

"Well, we've got this deployment coming up, and Tony's things are hopefully going to settle down here in the next thirty days or so, I hope. I don't know. I'm sort of thinking maybe I will get out. What about you, Tyler?"

"I'm thinking the same thing. I mean, I don't have as much overall time in length of service like you do, but I think we're done. I've got the kids to think of and other things I want to do."

"I've been thinking a lot about the Bone Frog group. You know that they asked me again when I was up there."

"Of course they did. We'd make great additions to their operation. They've got some good solid guys on their team too. I'm just not sure what their deal is all about."

"One thing that's kind of a deal breaker for me is that they're up in the Pacific Northwest. I want to spend as little time up there as possible. I mean, there're parts that are beautiful, and there's a lot of just gorgeous scenery and lakes and rivers and fishing and hunting. I used to really enjoy all those things, but I want to stick to things that are a little closer to home and where I want to live. Plus, Gretchen and the girls love San Diego. I couldn't take that away from them. And I told Kelly it would be a deal breaker for me if they stayed in Portland. We'll see what they do."

"Well, I'm in the same boat, Trace. And I will seriously look at whatever you look at, brother. Kate's the same way. She wants to stay here. She loves the community and the wives, and it's just something that's hard to see when you're not on the teams. All the guys training and you run into them at parties and things, and I know I'd miss it, Trace. That's the thing I fear the most. What if I get out and I get totally bored with life?"

"Well, that's why I'm thinking maybe staying with the Bone Frog group is a good alternative. We are men of action. We don't just wait for the world to fall apart. When we're called or compelled to go forward, we do. That's what a good man does. He protects the innocent. I'm not so sure I could work for anybody except someone like their team. I've sort of lost my trust in certain individuals, if you get my drift."

"Oh, I feel the same way. I think the public does too. It's getting to be pretty crazy out there. But we have to be at the ready, and I guess, if we were private, we could pick and choose what we do. And that's different than being on the teams. But thank God for the teams. Without them, look at where we'd be at."

"Yep, we need them. And there's a lot of good talent that's leaving, pursuing other things. It's good training for whatever, but once you're a team member, you're a team member. You could lead a warehouse full of technicians or a computer lab anywhere. You know how to lead and how to be part of something bigger than you are. It is just a question of finding the right things that stimulate all your juices, you know? Balancing your age and your physical abilities with that wonderful thumping of your heart when you're doing something dangerous."

"I know. Remember when we used to almost not be able to sleep at night because we were so anxious for the next day to start a mission?"

"Yep, I do. Those are some of my best memories, Tyler. And I am glad I stayed in, even with all the problems I had with Shayla. We all run into these personal things that we get involved with, and sometimes it takes guys off track. I'm glad I stuck it out, and look what I got. I got Gretchen and the girls. I found my new north. And maybe that's what has got to me. I feel like they're paying the price for my being gone so much. I'd like to be around more. Lord knows they need the protection."

"Right. About that. I think about it every day." Tyler wiped down the machine. "Let's grab some grub. Okay?"

"Nah, let's do another five miles down the beach first, and then we'll get some food," answered Trace.

Tyler and Trace wound up at the Rusty Scupper, getting their usual cheesy scrambles, hooking up with several of the other team guys who frequented the restaurant early in the morning when they were off.

Every time Trace walked into the Scupper, he saw the line of Navy SEAL pictures, men who had forfeited their lives for their cause, young men, mostly, looking like high schoolers, handsome and brave, standing guard for their SEAL photos. They bore their Tridents proudly, looked clear-eyed, and stared straight at the camera. Trace could see the courage in their souls as he studied the pictures of the fallen warriors. One by one, he gave his respects to each of them, some who he knew personally, some with stories that he'd heard, and several new ones he'd never met and regretted that.

Tyler walked silently behind him as they maneuvered through the gauntlet of history behind the bar.

They situated themselves in the corner, which was often the place where several of the SEAL Team 3 members would congregate. They'd been out in the sun so didn't want to sit outside on the patio where the barbecue was and the fire pit, and this was still early morning so he needed his breakfast in silence and in the dark.

When their order arrived, Tyler broached a couple of questions they hadn't discussed before.

"What do you think is going to happen with Tony?"

Trace put his fork down and thought about it for a second. "Sven told me something that kind of sums up my fear. I wouldn't say that I expect this, but it is a fear."

"What did he say?" asked Tyler.

"He said he didn't think Tony was long for this world. I really don't want that to happen, for the girls' sake."

He stared into Tyler's eyes and saw agreement there. "I'm conflicted. I wish I was never tasked with helping him, but it was what I had to do, and now I'm conflicted because Sven has inserted himself so deeply into Tony's affairs. I just don't know how it's all going to end."

"Well, don't worry about Sven. He's solid. I mean, I don't think anybody could get to him even if it was something bad."

"I'm not sure he knows what's coming. This Organization is super bad, and they don't really have any code. It's not like a family. It's like an amoeba or a flesh-eating something that preys on society, sucks the blood out of them, takes their treasure, and discards detritus. It's an evil group of people. It's too much for one man or even one group to go after. It would be years taking them down. And I fear that all Sven has done is substitute himself for Tony. And I'm here to tell you Tony's not worth it."

"Except he is your wife's ex and the father of your girls," said Tyler.

"That's true, and that's why I got involved in the first place. But Sven is committing funds as well as manpower. He very clearly wants me out of it, but I can't let Sven take that risk in my place."

"But we've got the deployment coming up, Trace. You forget your job."

"And that's why I'm conflicted, Tyler. It's my job, agreed. But I'm worried about what's going on at home. And I never used to feel like that. It's like each time I go away, I worry more and more about the people I'm leaving behind."

"You better talk to Kyle about that, Trace. You know what he's going to say. He's going to say if you start thinking about it, worrying about it, then it's probably time to get out. He's going to tell you that, Trace. Do you want to hear that?"

"Not yet. But I'm getting closer, Tyler. I would just

never forgive myself if something blows up while we're gone. I'm hoping and praying Sven can get this thing put to bed. I don't want it hanging over everybody's head while we're halfway across the world."

"I think you need to have a little more confidence in Sven and his capabilities. And it's not like he doesn't have a team. He's got Bryce, several SEALs from Team 5, and a couple of San Diego detectives and policemen, a couple of Marines, and some group guys. He's got a good crew behind him. If he needs it. And Kelly, well, she's still got weight, and they're smart, Trace. They have a lot more resources than you or I have, even being on the teams."

"Yeah, I agree. I just don't like that he's investing some money in Tony's recovery. Because Tony isn't good for it. He's not going to pay him back."

Tyler put his arm on Trace's shoulder. "Look, man, it's better that Tony owes Sven than owes those animals in The Organization. Take it from me. It's a much better place for everybody if that happens. Because Sven knows how to fight back. Tony? He'd just get mowed under. And you know how you'd feel about that."

CHAPTER 12

C LOVER ARRIVED HOME, loaded with bags of gifts she had bought for her two sisters, Gretchen, and Trace. Jack struggled at first getting things out of the car, but he brought up the rear with additional bags, leaving their luggage behind. Gretchen noted he didn't complain with all the stuff he had to carry, and it appeared he let Clover spend what she wanted on things to bring back. She smiled.

"Oh, so great to see you, sweetheart," she said as she hugged her daughter. "You look absolutely wonderful, a little sunburned, but you look fantastic, Clover!"

Gretchen saw the twinkle in her eyes, the happiness that was so much a part of Clover's spirit now blooming in her new life as a married woman. She hugged her son-in-law as well. "Thanks for taking good care of her."

"No problem. She's easy to please. A little bit of

sunshine, some margaritas, some beach time, some snorkeling, walks on the beach, a lot of talking. It was wonderful, the perfect honeymoon. Very laid back too," he said with a chuckle.

"What was the highlight of the trip?" Gretchen asked.

Angie joined the group, and the excitement accelerated again as she gave Clover a full body slam with the two dancing up and down. Eventually, everyone sat down, and Gretchen served some ice water. "You want something else, Jack?"

"I think I'd like a coffee if you've got any made. I am kind of weary from the flight and time difference. I'll take a nap this afternoon, but I'd like some coffee now."

"Coming up."

Clover shouted across the room as Gretchen ground coffee and prepared the French Press. "We loved the waterfalls, and there were some beautiful hiking trails up at the North Shore. They're kind of dangerous when it's wet and slippery, but the views are outstanding. There's no way you can get to those places except on that hike. And the snorkeling at the Ke'e beach at the most north portion of the island, that was beautiful, and the Waimea Valley, oh, it was all so gorgeous. All the rain we got. I actually didn't even mind it at all," reported Clover.

"Trace and I loved it there too. I'd like to go back someday. Maybe for our anniversary sometime," said Gretchen.

Jack added, "There was a cute little needlepoint store we ran into. Clover, you have that package?"

She dug through her bags and handed Gretchen a thin, pink paper sack. Inside was a hand painted needlepoint canvas. She was overcome with its beauty and the thoughtfulness of the two of them. Her eyes watered up.

"This lady is eighty-something years old, and she just sits there on the beach in her bare feet and paints these canvases for this needlepoint shop. They're really beautiful. All Hawaiian scenes. You'd love it there, Mom. I know you would, as soon as you can get back."

"This is beautiful. I'll work on this one next." Gretchen wiped her cheeks.

Clover pulled aside a package for Rebecca, handing it to Gretchen. "I'm not sure when I'll see her again, but, if you could give this to her from us, that would be great."

And then Clover handed Angie a package of the same size. Angie tore it open with gusto, and it revealed a long, beautiful flowered dress with a ruffled edge.

"These are traditional Hawaiian muumuus, made by a local seamstress. She only makes these, her own creation and design, and you see people wearing them all the time. But they are certified 100% Hawaiian made. Even the material is patterned and dyed there on the islands using organic local dyes. You'll want to wash it the first time in cold water, maybe twice, and then you should be good to go."

"Thank you, Clover. I love it," said Angie. She danced to her bedroom to go try it on.

Gretchen handed Jack his coffee and asked him if he wanted cream, which he declined.

"Where's Trace?" he asked.

"He's back, came back last night, and had a successful trip up to Portland. He'll be back for a while, and then he leaves on deployment in a few weeks. So they're getting ready for that. He's out doing a workout with Tyler."

"How is your project coming, Mom?"

"Have you got news I don't have?" asked Gretchen.

Clover smiled. "I got a call from Aunt Kate. I'm sorry. I guess you don't know they made an offer on this building, and it got accepted."

"Really? I didn't *know* that. She didn't *tell* me."

"Well, she offered me a job, Mom, and she wants me and Angie to help her with the cooking school and helping set up the catering business. Along with you, of course. But she wanted to make sure I didn't feel obligated or forced into doing it. She wanted to make sure it was something I wanted to do, so that's why she called me direct."

Gretchen was a little miffed that Kate hadn't let her know, but she understood her sister's tactics. Her sister knew Gretchen would be overly protective of Clover, and she understood why she wanted Clover's permission first before it was discussed further. But Gretchen still didn't like it. She attempted to cover up her disappointment at having been left out of an important decision.

"Well, it's one thing to tell her that my girls are all excited, but I understand she needed to check it out for herself. There's a lot of planning going on, but it's such an exciting project, and I'm so glad they got the building. We were over there yesterday, and it looks like somebody's already started to paint it."

"Well, I didn't know that. But anyway, she called me in Hawaii just so you know. And I told her I'd see what I could do. I didn't want it to interfere with school, and she didn't want that to happen either. But we're going to work out some hours that will allow me to do both. But there are a few little changes that are going to happen here, and I just wanted to let you know some recent news."

Gretchen sat up straight just as Angie danced into the room with her new dress.

"I love it. I absolutely love it!"

"Come have a seat. Your sister's about to tell us something," said Gretchen.

Clover took Jack's hand, and they looked at each other, the love between them emanating brightly. "Mom, we just found out we're pregnant."

"Wait a minute? You haven't even been back a day, and you already know you're pregnant?"

"I know. It shocked us too! We were snorkeling, and I stepped on a sharp piece of shell. We had to go to the emergency room to have it checked out, or that's what the concierge recommended. While we were there, they took a blood test, and I guess one of the things I'd mentioned to the doctor was that I had been kind of stressed and I hadn't had a period for a couple months. Well, the doctor went ahead and did a pregnancy test on me, which I was okay with. And it was positive. We're going to have a baby in about seven months. I guess we weren't careful enough."

Gretchen was shocked.

Angie ran over to her sister and gave her a big hug and fell into Jack's arms as well. "Oh my gosh. Oh my gosh. I'm going to be an aunt. I'm going to be an aunt!"

Gretchen was delayed in giving Clover her response, lost in thought about all the repercussions of this news. She hadn't quite figured out how she felt about it. She hugged her and hugged Jack and then took back her seat. "So how is this going to affect your schooling? And now this new job with the project? You've got a lot on your plate, Clover. And, Jack, what about your schooling? I mean, how's this going to affect everything?"

Jack started slowly, "Well, we're delighted, and we can't wait. I'm going to continue and see if I can double up on my schooling and get it finished early, or get as much done as I can before the baby arrives. You need to know, Mrs. Bennett, I want Trace to help me train for the Teams. Clover and I have talked about it, and I'll get my degree in case things don't work out, but I think—maybe a year from now—I'd like to try out."

Things were piling up on Gretchen faster than she could deal with. She felt herself floundering, in an emotional freefall.

"But, with a new baby at home, you want to be gone for all those important firsts?" Gretchen knew she was beginning to show her worry and concern. "How are you going to do all this?"

"Mom, you always said to trust you, to trust in life, and this is one of those times when you have to trust me. I think I know what I'm doing. I can finish my degree before the baby's here and still work part-time for Aunt Kate, you, and Deirdre. I'd really like to be involved in that. And I'll give up my coaching. I could turn that over to Angie and Rebecca if they'll take it."

Angie nodded enthusiastically. "Rebecca and I

would love to!"

Gretchen hadn't even considered this was a possibility. All of a sudden, she thought about all the moving parts—Trace leaving for Africa, Tony and his problems, now Clover being home and pregnant. What else could happen? She was filled with doubt and didn't want to rain on her daughter's parade, so she smiled and tried to show a united front.

"Sweetheart, if anybody can do it, you can. I believe in you. And Trace and I will support you however we can. I'm so happy that you've returned. And I'm so glad I'm going to be able to watch as your pregnancy grows and to be part of this new little one's development. New project, new life in the family, it's all good, Clover."

But Gretchen knew, inside, her worries were forming a dark cloud. This wasn't just going to be a change for Clover and her husband. It was going to cause an epic shift with all of them, the whole family. She was going to have to get ready for even more, even though she already thought they were on overload.

But with Trace, somehow, they'd pull it off.

CHAPTER 13

T RACE'S DEPLOYMENT TO North Africa and the Canary Islands came up as an emergency deployment. Kyle took with him twenty-five of the team members, since this operation was going to be carried out in various waves.

The State Department was concerned about a human trafficking operation that had just been discovered in the Canaries, which appeared to be rapidly growing in scope. There were questions about the national origin of the organizers, and the SEALs were tasked to go in and see if they could get intel, evidence of either Russian or Chinese assets being used to support this cause.

This particular mission wasn't a rescue but a fact-finding task in order to determine what, if anything, needed to be done. The fact that a huge number of new immigrants were sighted arriving at several ports in the islands and seen leaving in various crafts, including private jets—to parts unknown—was of concern to State. Due to the fact that there had been some unrest on the Canaries recently, Kyle got permission to bring a larger team than normal. There was always the possibility they would have to move on to the west coast of Africa. There were also military skirmishes spreading through Nigeria, parts of Benin, and Niger, as well as other parts of north and west Africa.

Trace was almost grateful for the new mission, since it took his mind off of the problems with Tony. In the transport, as they bumbled along across the Atlantic in the huge, very uncomfortable airplane, he thought about how he loved this part of the mission, the anticipation of the action, even though it was hot, noisy, and mind-numbing. Everyone went into their own space while they traveled. Everyone silently geared up and checked what they brought and made sure they were prepared for whatever the situation, listening on their devices, meditating, sleeping, or doing whatever they had to do to get their mindset into the game and flow of the mission, depending on their specialty. It was the quiet before the storm. Hopefully, the entire mission would be quiet. At least that's what Trace wanted.

He barely had a chance to congratulate Clover and Jack on their honeymoon, celebrate their news, and try on the aloha shirt that the two of them had bought him. It was adorned with palm trees and bright plumeria blossoms. He didn't want to tell them that the shirt was a tiny bit small, but he planned to wear it anyway when Clover was around. He'd beefed up these last few months working out, being helpful and active support to Gretchen and the girls, planning the wedding, probably overeating, and for sure overdrinking.

But he'd shed some pounds during this op since it was going to be hot and they would be eating on the run, not full sit-down meals. Often, in times like these, he would practically fast, if he was hydrated. It was better if he worked on an empty stomach than a full one.

He loved the glow in Clover's eyes and face, how Jack attended to her every need. And he was excited about the prospect of a new little one in their family. Unlike Gretchen, and she'd told him her reservations, he was pleased with the news. He thought Jack would make an excellent father. Trace planned on spoiling the dickens out of the new little one as well.

Kyle asked him to sit next to him so they could have a private conversation. It was difficult to do with the noise of the engines so loud.

"I just want to say in advance that I hesitated bringing you along on this mission, Trace, because of everything that's going on at home. You understand that there's no going back, even if something goes sideways?" Kyle asked.

"Yes, I got it. I appreciate it, sir. I'm all good. We've got another week or so before the escrow closes on Tony's house and the money gets delivered. Thankfully, Sven is involved. Never meant to do that to him, but, in hindsight, I'm glad I did."

"Damn straight. That was a good choice. Otherwise, you'd be wanting to stay home. I know you would. And I know you have some big choices coming up, Trace. Things I'm sure you don't want to mention. Let me just say, I want you here as long as you can be. I need you. I need experienced men, mature men who understand what this business is all about."

"Well, thank you, sir." He wasn't sure how to continue.

"You need to tell me anything now?" Kyle asked.

"Not the time, Kyle." He searched for something else to share and then found it. "Gretchen and I talked about me not checking my phone so often, and she's not going to bother me unless it's absolutely necessary. I plan to be fully present, Kyle, focused on what needs to be done, no matter what. Besides, it's really in Sven's hands, and I think he'd do a hell of a lot better job than I ever would anyway."

"Well, I'm not going to say that, but, frankly, you'll get no argument out of me. Sven's a standup guy. I wish he could get his citizenship taken care of, and I wish the Navy could have his butt on my team but that's not for Sven."

"He's an independent, sir. He's made for what he's doing now. He travels, he likes to roam, and he doesn't like to be tied down."

"Roger that. I'm just glad he's one of the good guys and he's on our side," said Kyle.

"He's a formidable enemy to any who try to destroy freedom."

They landed on Gran Canaria, and, before several of the team members were transported off island, Kyle called a meeting. Shortly, they'd be split up into three different compounds with groups of eight to ten men in each. Senior guys were embedded with each group so that those individuals could talk. Trace was put in the same camp as Kyle, so his leadership responsibilities would be minimal. But Cooper went over to one of the islands, and Tyler was tasked with leading another group at Tenerife. Fredo and several other long-termers were also sent to Tyler's group so he was provided with lots of assets.

When they got situated in the house that had been procured for them, Kyle gave the whole group an overview before the others were transported by ferry to their particular locations.

"This is a little bit different than some of our ops, fellas, in that we're supposed to be Uncle Sam's eyes and ears. We have some State Department help, but they'll be sort of invisible, on the sidelines. We aren't going to have as much direct and no on-the-ground communication with them. What we're supposed to do is look into this rapidly-growing smuggling operation that appears to have been formulated taking refugee ships from North Africa. Most of these are people who have traveled great distances, perhaps from Nigeria or more the interior of Africa, and they have secured paid passage to the coast where they take dinghies and arrive in the Canaries. It's a bounty system, similar to the operation going on at the U.S. southern border, with boat captains ferrying across migrants seeking to immigrate to the Canaries for probably no good reason. Maybe to participate in the human trafficking ring, the drug trade, or possibly to begin forming a standing militia that could be imported anywhere around the globe."

Kyle took a couple of minutes while the group took note of his message.

"Also, some of the larger ships are carrying human cargo. If we find one of those, we have authorization to stop it and then call in the Navy to board, unless they're being escorted by the Civil Guard."

"That's actually happening?" asked Jameson.

"Just what the rumor is. But, short of seeing actual evidence of human smuggling, we're interested in picking up stories and finding out who the leaders are, who's directing them, and who on the islands are supporting them. They can't run an operation without local support. We're supposed to find out where that's coming from."

Kyle showed the terrain of all of the islands and what they suspected was taking place in the various areas. "You have ship building over here. There's also a small factory we think is storing arms, but we are to check that out to be sure. Tyler and your group— you're going to be doing that. I want pictures, and I want names of people who come and go regularly. I want to know who owns the facilities if you can find out, and I want to know if any civilians like local police or militia are involved. That also would be helpful to the State Department."

Armando had a question. "Kyle, I need to ask you … Why is it that State doesn't use its own assets or the CIA to look into this? Why are we being tasked with this?"

Kyle had an answer for that and acknowledged Armando's question. "It's too dangerous, Armando. Things have just gotten to be a tinderbox over in Africa. We are not involved militarily except for some support staff and a SEAL Team. We have some operators embedded with the UN forces covertly. But they're not hardened, high quality assets, and we really don't want the diplomats or the CIA to get involved in a war. The diplomats aren't armed generally, and they don't have the ability to use force if it's necessary. That's why we're tasked with it."

Fredo asked another question. "I thought we're not supposed to engage?"

"Only if acted upon. Only in a dire emergency, to save one of our own. I'm not even sure we'd be justified in acting if it was a local person's involvement. I don't think we can do a rescue. At least we haven't been cleared for that. We're not supposed to start a war. We're supposed to report on what the status is before our government decides what approach they're going to take. It may be that there will be no military force at all, only economic. It may be that it goes through diplomatic channels. We don't know. But they need information that only we can get, and that will help them come up with a plan that works."

Trace had an idea. "What if we find local officials are compromised?"

"That's a very real possibility, Trace. In that event, we report and then we ask for solutions. We may just report and go home. I'm hoping it'll be something like that, that the gift of our intelligence will be enough to go on, so we don't get embroiled in a firefight. I really don't expect and don't want to do that."

One of the newer SEALs asked, "So how are we going about this? I mean, we're all on different islands doing different things. How do we communicate with each other? What happens if everything's coordinated with the traffickers going from one island to the next to the next? What happens if we see there's a direct correlation between all of these groups?"

"That's a good question, son. Your seniors will all communicate twenty-four seven. You report to your team leader. And it's definitely possible they are all connected. And that's part of our job. We sure as heck want to know what we're walking into before we do it. You don't want to hit the hornet's nest before you know how many are inside, right?"

"We usually do a lot of beach time, some cooking, we play a lot of cards, and minimal drinking, but some," said Coop.

"I'm going to say less on the drinking side, please. We're sometimes surrounded by people who don't drink, so you've got to remember that. That said, we are just American tourists, just a bunch of guys getting together to go fish or go play around. If we happen to go into some seedy bars and get firsthand information, so be it. That's what we do. We just be typical idiot American men. That's what they think of us, so that's how we'll play it."

Over the next two days, the team on Gran Canaria broke into groups of threes and fours, never less than three, and wandered the streets, oftentimes changing up who walked with who. When they got back to their mother house, they compared notes. Several of the men had been propositioned for prostitution, even offered underage girls, which was not uncommon in this region of the world. Those places that seemed to harbor individuals in that trade were noted, and a map was created. They set up a program of checking out those areas at different times of the day, even late at night, routinely changing up the guys, sending them out for one or two drinks and then pulling them back and sending another group later. It was like a scatter approach, a hit or miss operation, just to see what they could snag, kind of like throwing the net out to get fish bait for catching the bigger fish later on.

One of the guys in Tyler's group actually made contact with a hostess who had a whole house full of teenage girls, all of them Black, not native Canarians.

Kyle instructed them to send it up the chain and await the response before they did anything. Of course, they were asked to keep their distance until an okay was given.

On Gran Canaria, which was the seat of several government offices, a trio of the team members began a friendly conversation with several of the Guardia Civil officials, who seemed to be honest and talkative. The team members hesitated before they brought up anything about drugs or girls, wanting to see if the officials would bring it up to them first.

Later, Kyle asked the SEALs to find the Guardia Civil gentlemen to ask about their safety, if they wandered through the streets and looked for items to take home to their girlfriends and wives, if it was safe for them to travel in twos and threes, and if they were susceptible to smuggling or robbery.

The Guardia Civil were quite proud of the fact that they had greatly decreased the amount of drug smuggling, telling them so, in broken English.

In Spanish, Carlos, one of the newer SEALs, asked the police, "What about girls? Not for us, but if we brought our girlfriends or daughters, are they safe here?"

The local police all gave them the answer, in English, they expected to get. Yes, it was very safe there.

One of the guards offered, "The girls who are put into prostitution here have been smuggled in from other areas. We look for those people too, as they are breaking the law and making our shores less safe. Generally, the tourists and the population of Gran Canaria are safe from these people. They run houses for tourists or as a stop-off point for European and United States' destinations. But as far as girls and wives and daughters escorted by men, they would not be touched. It's sort of a code amongst the traffickers," the guard said.

"Where are these people from who do this?" Carlos asked.

"They come from all over. We have Russians, Ukrainians, people from Albania, Mauritania, Algeria, and several from Africa. African girls are the easiest, I think, to smuggle. They're often paid. They pay their parents to steal them. Or warlords, who capture families, kill the men and sell the women and children. Horrible business," the guard answered.

Carlos indicated to them that it was the same between the Mexican and U.S. border.

"You should not have a problem here as long as you are not dealing with drugs or girls. We want you to come to our islands and spend your money, have a great vacation, enjoy our beautiful blue waters and our lovely beaches and our culture. We have much in the way of culture, and we are like a bridge between Europe, Africa, Portugal, and Spain. A mixture of the whole world. We have a rich history of piracy and smuggling, but old traditions die hard. Things are much tamer now. We have order," the guard said.

After the SEALs made it back to their rented house, they sat around the pool, finishing their dinners, and talking about the day.

One of the Guardia Civil they had spoken to earlier showed up at the front door. This indicated, of course, that someone had followed them home. Carlos spoke to the gentleman and brought him inside the kitchen where Kyle and Trace were conversing. They didn't invite him outdoors to see the others.

"Please do not be alarmed. I'm one of the good guys," he said.

Trace wasn't sure he trusted him.

"Just in case you are doing something that is counter to the kidnappers and pirates who *do* frequent these islands, I'm available to be your resource."

"Why would you think that? And why would you put yourself out like that?" Kyle asked.

"I had a good friend who was working for the United States government and for the government in Spain. He was paid informant money, but, unfortunately, his status was discovered. He was murdered nearly a year ago now. He was my best friend. In his name, I would be agreeable to helping you find whomever it is you're looking for."

Carlos asked him how he took them to be anything other than just American tourists.

"I see the tattoos. I see the way your arms and shoulders are, the way you move. You gentlemen are trained, physically trained, and—just by watching you walk down the street—I can see there's something different about you. Most everybody who is attuned to that can tell the same. I will warn you, though, don't try to do anything on this island. The police have the backing of many of the kidnappers and money behind it. They're bought off, and they will disappear you. It's a very dangerous situation. I would not ask these questions unless you know who you're talking to. But I will help you all I can."

He shook hands with Carlos, and then Kyle stepped up, looking him in the eyes.

"I'm the leader of this group, and I don't deny those assumptions but won't agree with them either. I need to get your contact information. Do you have a secure line to discuss these things?" asked Kyle.

"Just my cell."

"Not secure enough."

"I have nothing else, sir."

"Then we'll get you something, but what about your family?"

"My family has gone to the United States. It is no longer safe for them here. I am waiting here for my mother's hospital operation. And then I will be escorting her to the States. I am not going to return, but the Guard does not know these plans. I can help you in the meantime, if you can get me some form of communication. That's why I came in person and alone."

"So be it. We'll get you that."

After he left, Kyle asked for and received word a set of phones that could be used on the island would be dropped by drone from one of their naval ships about twenty miles away. It would enable Kyle and the informant, Guerrero, to speak personally without interference. It was an untraceable number and had satellite coverage that was secure, untraceable.

They delivered the phones in a package at a predetermined drop-off in the city park downtown. Later on the next evening, Guerrero telephoned Kyle and let him know that he got the phone and that there was going to be a new shipment of young girls coming in the next day, and they'd been asked to not board or interfere with the cargo ship as it came in.

"You have the ship name and the time of arrival?" asked Kyle.

"Yes, sir, the Margarita Malaga." He gave the arrival and pier information.

"Roger that. We aren't going to interfere, so you will not be compromised in any way, but we are going to let the Navy know. Anything else like this you get, you let us know. Okay?"

"Will do. Is this worth some money to you?"

"I'm not a purser, Guerrero, but I'll see that something comes your way. We will let you know when we drop something off."

When Kyle relayed all of this to the State Department, he was told a package would be dropped off on the beach at midnight and given coordinates. It was to be given to the official to encourage him to keep the intel flowing.

Kyle placed the small envelope under the seat of the couch in the Hotel Don Pablo, on a public veranda located on the second-floor balcony off of the bar. It would be easy for Guerrero to get in there, pick up his package, and leave without being seen.

Similar pieces of information were collected from the other two groups. The name of the house owner—the madam of the young girls from Africa—was discovered and relayed. She was a recent Russian immigrant herself with experience running houses all over the world for various oligarchs and warlords.

A warehouse full of guns and drugs was located on Tenerife, not more than about two blocks from the famous beaches. All this information was relayed to the State Department. They were to wait the next few days to see if further action was required.

Trace asked for and was given permission to call home. He wasn't able to reach Gretchen, but he left a nice, long message. He missed her, he missed seeing Clover and the other girls, and he told her everything was safe, that he was good, and that they were fulfilling their duty and their promise, but, so far, no live action. He asked her to be patient and hoped that he'd be home soon.

He lay in bed and looked up at the stars through

the window that night. He knew she was looking at a different set of stars when it turned night in California. He thought about the way they strolled on the beach there, the project they were working on, and all the things that were ahead of them at home. He hoped that Tony got his money settled, and he hoped that Sven was out of danger.

Now his job was to complete the tour and get his butt home, perhaps once and for all.

"Goodnight, sweetheart."

CHAPTER 14

"**G**RETCHEN! I'M IN trouble, really big trouble!" Tony said on the other end of the line.

Gretchen reared up from a sound sleep, glancing at the clock. It was nearly 2:00 a.m. "Why are you calling me?"

"Because I don't have anybody else to call. I've been trying Trace for the past hour, and he doesn't answer."

"That's because he's not here. Why are you calling Trace? I thought you had Sven helping you out?"

"Well, I don't want to get him involved. I didn't want to tell him."

"Tell him what?"

"I got busted. I got busted with someone I thought was a hooker. And I'm sorry to tell you this, but I got enemies here, Gretchen. I got to get out of jail. I got to get bailed out tonight. I'm afraid what's going to happen when people find out about it tomorrow morning."

"Wait a minute, Tony. You got money. You got money from the loan on the house. What's up with that?"

Tony mumbled something that didn't make sense to Gretchen. "Are you drunk, Tony?"

"Just a little, and, as far as the money, I'm not sure where it is."

The last part, he whispered into the phone, obviously trying to protect the information from others who might be waiting in line.

"I'm sorry, but there's nothing I can do. We're tapped out. There's just no money here for me to do that, and I'm not going to put any of our assets on loan until Trace is back here. I can't help you, Tony. You're going to have to call Sven."

"Do you understand what I'm saying? I'm in danger, Gretchen." He was slurring his words and getting more and more emotional by the moment.

"Tell me exactly what happened. You picked up a prostitute and then got arrested?"

"Well, she wasn't really a prostitute. She was a decoy. And I propositioned her, and, well, you know, she took all the money I had. I mean, I've got more. I just can't remember where I put it. It's somewhere in the house. Maybe the tenants took it, I don't know. But I'm in a jam, and my biggest problem right now is there are people who, as soon as they find out I'm in jail … I'm going to be toast, just toast."

"Not to mention what Sven's going to do to you when he figures it out."

"Don't bring up Sven."

"Why not? He was your guardian angel, Tony. All you had to do was stop being a jerk, stand up and be a man for a change. There's absolutely nothing I can do, and calling me was a mistake."

Just then she saw Angie at the doorway, then make her way into the bedroom and sit down on the bed next to her. She was sick that Tony's daughter was going to be privy to all this information. But they'd already had somewhat of a dose of reality. Gretchen figured she might as well just finish it off.

"You know your daughter's sitting here, next to me, and she's wondering why you would call me at two o'clock in the morning. Should I tell her that you tried to—"

"Don't tell her!" yelled Tony.

Gretchen had half a mind to just hang up on him, but, in looking at Angie's sad eyes, she thought better of it. "I'll try to reach Sven, but that's the only way you're going to get out of there. First of all, I'm not in Portland. You could just have them escort you to the house to pick up your money. It must be there."

"I'm not in Portland. I'm in San Diego."

"San Diego? What the *hell* are you doing here?"

"I needed a break. I just needed to go back, and, well, I have a couple friends here, and I couldn't find them, and I thought maybe I'd run into somebody I knew, one of Trace's friends or Trace or—or *you* maybe, or somebody downtown. So I just hung out there, and I guess I had too much to drink."

"Tony, you can't just drop in on us here. We're not here for you any longer."

"She's my kid."

"She's fourteen, and you are to stay away from her. You aren't allowed unsupervised meetings or contact, Tony. You know that."

Tony was breathing hard into the phone. It sounded to Gretchen he was about ready to pass out.

"San Diego should be safer than up there," said Gretchen.

"No, it's not. I got word Sam had me followed. Somebody passed me a message and said Sam is after me. He's coming to get me. What the fuck do I do, Gretchen?"

"If he's going to bail you out, let him!"

"He'll kill me."

She nearly said the unthinkable, but didn't. "You call Sven. I'll try as well. Which station are you at?"

"Central North, I don't have the address, but I think he could find it. Do you think maybe you could come down and try to talk to these guys?"

"Hell, no. I'm not going to go do that. They're not going to listen to me anyway."

"Okay, well, at least I tried. Hey, Gretchen, I'm sorry about all this. I'm sorry about everything."

"You should tell your daughter. I'm done with you, Tony." She hung up the phone.

She sat there with her elbows on her knees, her face buried in her hands. She wanted to burst out crying, but, with Angie sitting next to her, she held it all in. Angie's sweet words helped her mood somewhat. She placed her arm around her mother's shoulder and drew her close.

"Mom, it's okay. Dad's a full-on creep. And he shouldn't ask you to go down to the station and bail him out."

"You heard all that?"

"Of course, I couldn't help but hear. He was yelling in the phone, Mom. I know you can't get hold of Trace, but do you have this other guy's number?"

She'd forgotten about Sven. "Yes, yes. Let me see—" She scurried through her room to find Trace's desk drawer and was hoping he'd have Sven's card. She saw Kelly Fielding's card and called it.

The line went to a disconnect message. Apparently, they'd changed numbers when Kelly had moved full-time to Portland. She looked at the card carefully to see if there was another number, and did find a cell. She dialed.

"Hello?" Kelly answered.

"Oh, Kelly, it's Gretchen, and I just got a call from Tony. He's in jail, for heaven's sake. He got arrested for picking up a police decoy for prostitution."

"Goddamn that guy. Boy, he's sure headed for the jaws of death, isn't he, Gretchen? Let me go find Sven. I think he's sleeping downstairs."

"I'm so sorry, Kelly, but I don't know who else to ask."

"Well, he's supposed to call us. I wonder what happened."

"Well, Tony was just being Tony, right?"

"Hang on a sec. Let me go get Sven."

Gretchen heard her feet tapping the stairs, then footsteps as she ran to the living room where the television was playing. Kelly woke Sven, who had probably fallen asleep on the couch.

She turned off the TV and, once Sven had collected himself, he grabbed the phone. "Gretchen, what's up?"

"Tony's down here in San Diego, and he got picked up for solicitation of a prostitute, a police decoy. He's asking for money to bail himself out, and I don't have it. And I'm not going to go down there. It's just not right. I'm not going to do it."

"I wonder why the hell he went down *there*?"

"I don't know, but, anyway, I'm not sure what to

do. He said he's at the North Central Station. And he says he can't find the rest of his money."

"That asshole. After all the work we went through with all this stuff, and he's just blown his money again. I mean, how could he blow $25,000 in five days?"

"Because Tony is Tony, and he's extremely flawed."

"Can you get hold of Detective Mayfield? Maybe he can get some information and then call me back. Use this number." Sven gave Gretchen his direct cell.

"Okay, I'll try. If I don't reach him, then I'll text you his number and you can try. I just don't know who else to call. I mean, should I call Christy or what should I do? I don't want to bother Trace."

"No, don't call Trace. You have any reason to think Tony's in danger? I mean, maybe we should just let him sit there till morning."

"Well, he did say that Sam somehow got a message to him that he was after him or he was going to come get him or something like that, I don't know."

"Geez. So he sounded urgent, right?"

"Yes, he did. He was panicked. I've never heard him so frantic before."

"Okay, well, try to get ahold of Gus, and maybe he can do us a good one and get him isolated or put under special observation somewhere. At least until I can get down there and sort this out, but, geez, I feel like I've got a fourteen-year-old teenager who's driving without a license. I had no idea Tony was such a handful."

"Well, now you know what Trace has been going through. I'm just not sure why Tony keeps getting himself into these situations."

"Me neither, but if Tony wants to kill himself doing it I'm not going to stop him. It's just that now he's come closer to you and brought all this danger with him. That's not cool, Gretchen. You armed?"

"Of course I am."

"You lock all your windows and doors, and you get your guns out. Keep Angie with you at all times. Don't leave the house until I can get somebody over there to give you some protection. Okay?"

"Thanks, Sven. I really owe you."

"No, sweetheart, you don't owe me. Tony does. But, first, he owes an apology to you, your girls, to everybody. He's just maybe not redeemable. And I'm sorry to say that, but he's not worth all this effort we're having to go through just to keep him safe. I get him out of one mess and he jumps into another one."

"Thanks, Sven. I'm going to go load up, check the windows and doors, and try to go back to sleep."

"Well, keep your phone by you so we know you can reach us."

Gretchen and Angie ran around the house, making sure that every single window was closed and latched, that every door was bolted and dead bolted. She dug out two of Trace's guns, including his SIG Sauer, and loaded it, leaving an extra magazine on the nightstand just in case. She also got out his Smith & Wesson and did the same. Everything being checked and double-checked, she left one of the guns in the kitchen underneath her tea towels next to the stove. The other one she left upstairs in her bedroom. No matter which place she needed it, she'd have it on either floor.

Then she sat down on the couch with Angie by her side and gave Gus Mayfield a call.

"Gretchen? What's up, honey? Something wrong?"

"I'm sorry to bother you, but my ex, Tony, he's in jail down at Central North. He's gotten into some trouble with some gambling, and Trace and Sven have been trying to work it out. But he got busted for solicitation, and he's there, but he's scared that somebody's coming for him. He thinks somebody from Portland is after him, one of the criminals who lent him the money, who owns his gambling debts."

"Well, Trace is overseas, right?"

"Yes, everybody's over there. And I don't know when they'll come back. But you know their friend Sven was working with Tony to help get his debt paid off, and they were almost there. I mean, Tony has money coming in a week or so. They arranged it with this guy who Tony got into for a lot of money. They arranged it and all Tony had to do was just keep his nose clean until the house closed, until the guy could get paid off. I don't know why, but he came down to San Diego, and now he's in jail, and he's worried about some guy coming to get him. Sven asked me to tell you this to see if there's some kind of way he could be isolated someplace away from the rest of the population so nobody could mess with him?"

"Wow, let me see what I can do, but, boy, it's the wrong time of day for that. Let me call the station and see what they got on him, and I'll see if I know anybody there still. Most of my friends have retired now, so I don't have the clout I used to have, but I'll try."

"You don't have to call me back, Gus. Just give Sven a call. Here's his number." She gave him both Sven's cell and also Kelly's.

"I'll do what I can, and then I'll call Sven back. You go get some sleep. And, Gretchen?"

"Yes?"

"You got some protection?"

"Yes, sir, I do. And I'll use it if I have to. I got Angie here."

"Good girl, but be careful. I'll see if I can send someone over to help. I know a couple guys who sort of moonlight for the department. I'll see if one of them is available."

"Thank you so much."

Gretchen made sure all the lights were off, and she

and Angie waited upstairs, in the dark, sitting in the big, armed reading chair in the corner of their bedroom. They could see the full vista of the street below, and so far there was no traffic, no foot traffic either. They were going to have to be vigilant.

Angie finally fell asleep in Gretchen's bed, and, though her daughter was able to nod off, occasionally snoring, Gretchen was racked with fear. Her mind was going a million miles a minute. She was imagining all the things that could go wrong. When she thought things were put to bed, all of a sudden everything blew up again.

She began to realize that this was what it was like to have Tony as part of her life. And she'd bent over backwards to try to accommodate him for years when they were married, and, now that she was on a different path and safely tucked in the arms of Trace, Tony still wouldn't leave her alone, couldn't stay out of their lives. And he was going to threaten everything she held dear.

Even if she could reach Trace, she didn't want to interrupt him in the middle of an important mission or distract his focus. That wasn't right. And Tony had no right to bring that on either of them.

Hopefully, Gus could arrange for some protection.

Around 5:00 a.m., she saw a car drive up to the front, park, and turn its lights out. No one got out of the car, so she figured perhaps Gus had sent someone and was protecting the house. Oddly enough, after she saw the car, she relaxed and soon fell asleep.

Gretchen awoke, hearing the sound of breaking glass. It came from downstairs in the kitchen. Angie had been startled, as well, and was clinging to her.

"Mom! Mom, what is that? I'm scared."

"Shh, please be quiet. I don't know what's going on." She got up and put her finger to her lips, pointing to the door to show Angie to lock it behind her. In her nightgown and her bare feet, she quietly moved out onto the landing and then carefully walked down the stairs looking for whoever was there. The car in the front was gone, and, as she looked through several of the windows, she didn't see anyone wandering around the outside.

Suddenly, an arm snaked around her to grip her neck and shoulders. A dirty hand covered her mouth, and the cool metal barrel of a gun pressed to her temple.

"You be quiet, little lady. Everything will work out. We're going to go for a little ride."

Gretchen hoped that Angie would stay put. But no sooner did she have that thought when she heard her daughter's voice from the top of the stairs, "Mom? Mom, is that you? Are you okay?"

She closed her eyes and waited for the next horrible

thing to happen. Her thoughts raced, wondering what she should do. An image of something she'd learned in her self-defense classes popped up. Since both arms were up, one around her shoulder and mouth and the other to her temple, his belly was exposed. It was a risk, since he had the gun aimed at her head and could accidentally go off, but she was out of choices. She pushed the barrel of the gun away from her face with an open palm uppercut, then elbowed him as hard as she could right in the lower gut, which sent him reeling back, and the gun went off as he dropped it.

Angie screamed.

The morning light was beginning to come in through the windows, and Gretchen saw where the gun skittered across the granite floor to a corner in the kitchen. She scrambled to get it. He recovered himself and limped toward her as she turned around, aimed the gun at him, and told him to stop.

The man was small, but with his very fleshy belly, ruddy skin, and his angry demeanor, she was frightened to death. But she had to protect Angie. Aiming the barrel of the gun at his face, she said, "I know how to shoot this. You back up! You back up, and you go outside. I've got the police coming right now."

"That doesn't bother me at all. You and your daughter will be long dead by then." He still walked slowly toward her, step by step. "No need to make a scene out of this, Missy. You don't want to die. You don't want your daughter to die. All I'm looking for is a little bit of money."

"I don't have any money. I never have any money, thanks to my ex."

"Oh, we're going to take care of Tony too. Believe me, he's been a very bad boy. You know this though, right?"

As he stepped forward once more, she aimed and shot the floor right between his feet. This caused him to jump.

"Okay, I get your point. But you don't want things to end this way, do you? If you cooperate just a little bit with me, I promise you'll be safe. We'll even leave Angie here. She'll be safe and sound here, and your friends can protect her. I just need you to come with me to give a little extra insurance."

"Do you think I'm stupid? Do you really think I would do that?"

"Well, if you want to sacrifice Tony, if you want to tell that little girl up there that you made it so that her father will never come home, well, I guess that's your decision, right?"

Gretchen aimed carefully, her hands shaking. When he lunged at her again, she pulled the trigger, and the man fell to the floor, his head hitting the granite with a thud. Blood oozed out from his chest as he struggled briefly with his arms and then went limp.

CHAPTER 15

WORD CAME DOWN to the group on Gran Canaria that a shipload of new merchandise, meaning children but mostly young girls, was arriving at two o'clock in the afternoon. It was bold of them to off-board in the middle of the day, but there was transportation being arranged, from cars and buses to airplanes, for parts unknown. Part of their cargo had already been sold or committed and was going to be departing shortly after arrival.

State gave Kyle the go-ahead to conduct a raid and try to secure the merchandise, with the help of the rest of Team 3. It was not thought that the perpetrators would be expecting a raid, especially from a SEAL team.

The project escalated to "urgent"—or "red"—when it was discovered that a missionary worker and his family from Africa were among the group arriving by boat. The doctor had maintained a mission in Nigeria for one of the large church organizations in Holland, although he was an American. Somehow, the protection detail that had been arranged for him—and had been working for many years—failed. With all the recent changes in the governments in Nigeria and other countries nearby, it was somewhat tricky for these groups now who were not doing anything but humanitarian work, first aid, clinics, and of course Bible training in schools to operate. One by one, many of them were leaving. Some had been raided with loss of life.

Carter Solvang, from California, and his wife and four daughters were the perfect targets for a militia group and got swept up in the raid on their school. Over half of the cargo arriving was from this one school and the surrounding countryside.

Dr. Solvang was a U.S. citizen, as were all of his children, although two of them were born in Africa but maintained their U.S. status. Dr. Solvang's wife was Dutch but was a green card resident of the U.S. Except for fundraising tours, the Solvangs hardly ever returned to the U.S.

Kyle woke the team up early, and they began their preparations. The boys from Tenerife and the other outer islanders were brought in quickly by private jet and soon all twenty-five of them assembled at the Mother House on Gran Canaria where they were triple and quadruple bunked.

Kyle showed the picture of the missionary and his family. "He's, of course, going to stand out because he's white, and we don't know what his condition will be or the condition of any of his family, but they will be our first priority, as well as any women and children who are with them. State Department would like us to save them all, but we're not given exact numbers, so we'll have to play it by ear."

Trace had a question. "You got this information from State. But do you trust Guerrero with this as well? Might he have one or two Civil Guard who can assist us?"

Kyle shook his head. "I've been told not to reveal it to anyone. We could use the extra manpower, of course, but we're not going to bring in naval forces for any ready-action command at this particular point. The USS Bulkeley is trolling these waters as we speak, only for backup support, should it be needed. The guided missile destroyer is about fifty miles offshore in Las Palmas, away from the main shipping lanes."

Kyle continued, "Twenty-five of us should be able to get at least the missionary and his family out and several others. We'll have to figure out a drop-off point and time, and we'll be calling in to the Navy to have them provide that transport plane as soon as we know how many and when. Currently, we understand another support vessel is also due to arrive shortly, with other capabilities. They're all on standby and are going to head closer in our direction so they can provide quick aid if we need it. We also don't want to start a war with the presence of these ships."

Kyle paced a step before turning back to his men. "The cargo ship's registry is Mauritanian, and we do have relations with this country. It is believed that the cargo traversed the country, partially protected by local militia. But, before you jump to conclusions, you need to remember that this is a country that has not had a terrorist attack since 2011 and has cooperated with the United States for anti-terrorism and anti-slavery events. They also recently had a peaceful presidential election and a peaceful presidential transition after their current president was convicted of corruption. They are staging for a new election coming up soon. And the other thing you need to take into account is this Muslim country still allows slavery, those who own slaves can continue to own slaves and the children of those slaves are also considered the property of the owners."

Kyle said the word "owners" in finger air quotes.

The reaction among the men was swift, whispering various forms of disapproval.

"We believe they are not in favor of supporting terrorist groups who raid villages and capture. It's the institution itself of slavery, not the raiding and capturing, as they're trying to balance between peace and the stability of being a leader in the African continent. The U.S. is trying to help them with this transition, but there are dangerous hotspots. They're not going to want to intercede or do anything at all that will distance them from the rest of their African neighbors, who are increasingly becoming more and more militant and threatening.

"However, we are trying to negotiate a peaceful takeover of the ship and return of the slaves as best we can. We also have learned that Mauritania is aware of the missionary and his family, and, although they will not defend them, they will help see to it that they have found their way into our hands. At this point, though, they do not know it will be a SEAL force meeting them at the dock.

"Here's the rough part, gents. We are forced to work with a UN representative, which is the weakest link in this program. Not sure if we can trust the gentleman, but we have to work through him and his staff, our State Department says. On Gran Canaria, while treated almost like a separate country, they still are part of Spain and, thus, are part of NATO. It would be an embarrassment if a NATO ally were to harbor criminals operating in an already agreed-upon prohibited criminal behavior. But that doesn't mean that some of the Guardia Civil isn't corrupt and been paid off handsomely."

It was decided that a first wave of SEALs would attend to the surveillance of the port, confirm when the ship would arrive, and which pier it would dock at. Trace was part of that group, and, as soon as they received their instructions, he left with the rest of the team of ten to communicate back to Kyle at the Mother House.

They rode in cargo vans, which lacked windows and were somewhat of a hindrance as far as getting their bearings. There was a rear window which showed little of the pier and the dock works beside. They parked the van and left their gear inside, again posing as American tourists, even bringing along fishing poles that had been provided in the van to complete the ruse.

They split up into two groups on the pretense of looking to book a fishing boat, and, luckily, since most Grand Canarians also spoke English as well as Spanish, Portuguese, and some Arabic, they were able to inquire about the potential for a fishing charter. They didn't have to mention that they were a group of ten but looked for boats that were larger, perhaps in the vicinity of where a much larger ship like a cargo ship could be docked.

The intel they received confirmed a two o'clock docking of a large, repurposed cruise ship from Mauritania, the Margarita Malaga.

When the team returned to the Mother House, they had an unexpected visitor. Guerrero showed up with three of his men. Kyle was immediately alarmed and stopped them at the front porch.

"We come bringing you information about a ship arriving today. Many in the militia, the guard, have been tasked with helping transfer human beings to other transports quickly to avoid detection. We believe it is human smuggling cargo mainly but also drugs and gold."

Kyle was hesitant to invite him inside. The group stood outside the front door, with Trace and Armando at Kyle's side.

"Wait here." Kyle asked Armando to stay at the front door on the outside, while he placed his call to the Head Shed. "I'm going to call for guidance, see what we can do next. It looks like our cover is blown anyway."

He got on his sat phone and relayed the information. He was given permission to bring the group in, carefully watch them, and not let them leave or send communications elsewhere. They were asked to check their listening devices and what weapons they carried.

Kyle went outside with Trace and spoke to Guerrero.

"Okay, I've been given the green light, but you are

not to use your cell phones. In fact, we're going to confiscate them." Guerrero turned and gave instructions to his men who, one by one, gave them their cell phones.

"We're also going to have you searched, and I want to see what weapons you carry. I'm not going to confiscate the weapons, but I just need to know what kind of firepower we have. And, Guerrero, are you a hundred percent solid with all these people? I mean, I'm putting the lives of my men in your hands, so, if there is an ambush afoot here, if you don't know of something but something comes up, I expect you to let me know in time to save my men. This is way out of our normal protocol."

"I understand, sir. Lupe here is from my family, the cousin of my sister, and I have several others who I know from work experience. I have been paired with in the past. There's only one I don't know personally, but Lupe has recommended him and stands by him 100%. These men all, as well as myself, hope that we see the day someday when our government can function as a noncorrupt entity, free from Spain's influence and interference, and not make its money off of the piracy and trade that is out there."

"Okay. Well, we'll conduct the search and then we'll be on our way. You're to stay with our group at all times."

The men were brought into the house where several of the SEALs did a thorough search, examining their weapons and their extra rounds. The men had duty bags that most SEALs had as well, with extra equipment, long guns, and some small explosive devices, which impressed Kyle.

They were offered food and coffee, and, within thirty minutes, Kyle received the call that they were a go and to start heading down toward the pier.

Guerrero led the way, in his official civil guard vehicle. Trace sat in the Jeep beside him. In the seats behind them were two SEALs. Guerrero's other three men rode in two different vans with the rest of the group. It was a warm day already, the noontime beginning a hot streak that would last well until eight o'clock that evening. A brisk, hot wind floated down from the mountains and competed with the ocean breezes but gave little relief from the heat.

It was a workday, so people lined the streets in donkey-driven carts or go-karts—little lawnmowers with vans on them, as Fredo called them. People walked with bushels on their heads and rode e-bicycles, carrying bushels under their arms, or packed on platforms in the back. Frequently, they'd see a goat led by a child, but most of the animals that were headed for the marketplace downtown were chickens or ducks or pigs kept in cages.

"You people raise pigs here? With the high population of Muslims—" Trace started.

"Oh no, we are Muslim minority. But pigs are very well received here. Goats as well. But people with money will buy pigs. Better meat, easier to raise. Chickens, you know chickens get eaten all over the world. I don't much care for them," Guerrero added.

"How's your mother doing?" Trace asked.

"Thank you, she's in pain. She was due to have her surgery last Tuesday, but it was bumped for some particular reason. Here, people have things scheduled, but then it's set aside for a more high priority patient. Usually, it means a politician," Guerrero said without batting an eye. He kept his vision on the dusty road ahead.

"Is it chronic?"

"No, señor. She fell. She's been dealing with a fractured hip now for nearly eight days. Very painful."

"So what will the repercussions be for you with this action today?"

"Well, I think we will claim that you commandeered us. Perhaps it depends on what happens. But we are here as advisors, as guides to make sure there is as little bloodshed as possible. I think that is a worthy goal. You already had the information about the ship, it seems, so I didn't really give you anything new, but I will tell you that some of my brethren—no one in this

SECOND TIME LOVE

group—will be on the other side of the fence, and I must be careful."

He looked at the SEALs in the back seat who sat stoically and listened to everything he and Trace were saying.

"So what have the other men been told?" asked Trace.

"They have been told to not intervene, to not do anything unless something has happened that risks your life or you're being taken captive. Then we have to act, but we aren't going to do anything but support. We hope that support is worth something to Uncle Sam. We would like you to get your cargo and then leave the Canary Islands as soon as possible. That is the safest for all of us."

That was good enough for Trace. At last, they reached the docks. Several of the fishing trawlers they'd seen earlier had left, leaving a wide space large enough for a cruise ship to dock, if necessary. They were dropped off at a lot near that space where a small cantina and several other little vendor shops and a liquor store were located. Music was everywhere around the port, and Trace noted a line of workers waiting to unload cargo, all with iron wristbands, indicating ownership. There were also several independent loaders and hand trucks standing idle.

Guerrero parked his vehicle in a lot under the trees,

and the other two vans arrived next to him. Kyle grouped the men in teams, splitting in three different directions from the shadows, each taking up positions, armed with only handguns. Armando and a newbie named Armie stayed back at the vehicles. They were armed to the teeth with their long guns and scopes, and he was going to be in constant communication with Kyle in case something was needed.

Armando quickly found a local cantina and climbed up the back of it, holding onto the cistern, laying himself flat on the roof next to Armie, the other SEAL. They prepared their scopes and readied themselves for whatever was required. They could see through the branches of the trees, but the trees hid them from full view of the docks.

A horn blared in the distance, indicating a ship was approaching. And around the rocky pier, a large transport ship filled with containers slowly made its way into the harbor and docked broadsides at the pier. It was tied up for easy offloading. A hatch was opened, and a gangway was provided from the land side. Several officers, probably the harbormaster as well, came out to greet the ship captain and other officers who appeared on the gangway. They all cordially shook hands.

One of the officers signaled to a group of taxis and truck drivers to advance, and they did so, temporarily obscuring the entry. Kyle and the team moved in between the crowds beginning to arrive. Guerrero stood close by him. Trace stood behind them and whispered to Kyle, "How do we get the missionaries out first?"

"I'm going to have Guerrero request it. State sent me a printout that I can use. We'll see if it works."

Guerrero and Kyle made their way closer to the gate as passengers started unloading from the ship. Several private, paying customers came off first with luggage and helpers. They got into black Suburbans and took off. Over his INVISIO, Armando was tasked with getting pictures of all these VIPs exiting the ship. It hurt Trace to see these guys walk away to freedom without any repercussions, but that wasn't the prize they were looking for.

Finally, a group of young girls were let off, roped together through chains on their wrists. They were young, maybe ten, twelve years old, scared, and every single one of them barefoot. The crowd began to notice and whistle, some making sounds of objection. The girls were pulled off to the side and asked to sit on barrels and canvas bags that were stored, ready to be loaded.

Another group exited and joined the young girls, and then finally the missionary and his wife and children followed behind. Dr. Solvang appeared to be in relatively good shape, although he was sporting an injury to his eye or had incurred some kind of abuse about the face, but he walked normally, and he was allowed to hold the hand of his wife, who was also connected by chain to the children. They were herded to the right, next to the young Black girls, just as a large black bus arrived close by, presumably to take them to another location. Kyle dragged Guerrero forward and spoke to what he assumed to be the captain of the ship.

Trace stood nearby within voice range.

"Excuse me, sir. I have an official request from the State Department of the United States to release these prisoners." He handed the paperwork to the captain. Guerrero stood motionless, noncommittal, beside Kyle.

The captain glanced over it, frowned, and handed it to the representative from their harbor patrol.

Kyle got a quick response. "This has no jurisdiction here. This is not valid. These individuals are being transported of their free will to another location. They were evacuated from a war zone," the man said. His steely eyes bore into Kyle, and Trace was sure he got the same dose in return from his LPO.

"Then I shall have to inform the United States Navy, which is nearby, as you know, that you are being uncooperative. As a matter of fact, we are tasked with releasing all of these children and this missionary. We understand these were individuals taken not by choice, but by force, by violent force."

Kyle was good at this, Trace saw, and he had the attention of the captain and had earned the ire of the local official.

"As a NATO ally, you must honor the wishes of one of your own. The United States is a good friend. And we are good friends with the Mauritanians as well. It is our desire to continue to be so."

The ship captain nodded his head and revealed a tight smile.

"I am going to have to check with my superiors," said the harbormaster.

Kyle nodded and put the phone up to his ear, loudly declaring, "I'm going to check with mine. Perhaps you would like to speak to the captain of the Bulkeley, the guided missile destroyer? It's not more than twenty miles off your shore. Let me arrange this."

The official walked away with his ear to the phone, disappearing into the crowd.

The captain used this time to plead his case.

"I know nothing of this. I am paid to bring cargo in, and these passengers were bought and paid for."

Kyle assumed a stronger position, inhaled, and stood taller. "Were they purchased as people or was their passage purchased? I'm sure my Navy captain would like to know. We were told they were prisoners, involuntarily removed from their mission in Nigeria and transported across Mauritania to this ship. Perhaps my State Department needs to notify the embassy in Mauritania that your ship is carrying contraband, specifically United States citizens, beyond their will."

All of a sudden several vans with troops appeared, all with the Civil Guard insignia. Guerrero disappeared into the crowd, and Trace lost track of where he was. He was concerned that they'd walked right into a trap.

In the distance, Trace could see a helicopter was arriving. Kyle was still on the phone with the Navy when the harbor representative arrived. Noting the presence of the Civil Guard, the guard created a barrier between the public that was now growing in size and becoming increasingly curious and the offloaded passengers and cargo. Men sent to pick up material and deliver them into the city were objecting that they were being kept from doing their job. Lorry drivers and other workmen objected to the traffic jam created in the square next to the pier.

The public, including several local shopkeepers, started arguing with each other, and Trace could see that the groups that had been assembled were not homogeneous and were beginning to war amongst themselves such that it may begin a small riot. The whole area was destabilized.

Over his INVISIO, Trace heard the message from

Kyle, which got delivered to all the SEALs. "We have a bird arriving. No one move. Just stay together and keep track of each other. Guard your sidearms, and don't get arrested."

The sound of the helicopter blades increased, and Trace could see there were three helicopters, not one, arriving over the small mountain range that traversed the island. One landed just outside the crowd and the other two off toward the parking lot, fifty feet away.

Captain Ronald Higby from the U.S. destroyer, a thirty-year man whom Trace recognized from naval newsletters throughout the years, walked up with his two aides, dressed in whites, and pierced the crowd, headed straight for the captain of the transport ship. They shook hands. There was some discussion that Trace couldn't understand, but he found that Captain Higby did most of the talking, and the transport ship captain did most of the nodding. He turned to the steady line of cargo workers and stopped, halting the offloading of anything further. A large moan rose from the crowd as people became agitated. Of note was the fact that the helicopters did not shut down but continued while awaiting instructions.

Higby was blocked from seeing the missionary, but, very gently and firmly, his two aides removed the three gentlemen who were blocking access. Soon Captain Higby was shaking hands with the doctor and his wife.

He motioned for them and whispered something to the doctor. Then he gathered together the group of young girls, and they headed toward the helicopters. On his way past Kyle, he saluted. Kyle returned the salute.

The transport captain was nonplussed. The representative of the harbor had disappeared temporarily but soon ran to the gangway and tried to stop the movement of the missionaries.

Trace prevented him from getting closer to Kyle.

"You hold on a second there. I think we do have jurisdiction here, and, unless you want a hundred sailors pouring into this port engaging in some kind of protection detail against your men here, unless you want that or you want a bunch of SEALs conducting an operation which will not end well for you, I suggest you just sit back and cooperate. This wasn't anything you knew about. This was something we learned through our intelligence. You need to cooperate or Uncle Sam will be all over your butt."

The gentleman from the harbor looked Trace up and down and sneered, spat, nearly hitting his shoes. Trace stepped into him and grabbed his arm, putting a handcuff on it.

"Maybe you would like to be taken as well? We can certainly do that. You like to explain your existence to the crew of a naval destroyer?" He didn't put the handcuff on the other arm as Kyle stopped him and pushed Trace aside.

"You can see my men are rather touchy about the subject of hurting innocent women and children. I'm sure you will have future cargoes that will make up for this loss, but we are taking these people back to where they can return to their domicile. They have been kidnapped, and, unless you want to be named as an accessory, you need to back off and let it happen."

The harbormaster was no doubt seeing his profits evaporate. The lucrative day was turning dangerous for him and too risky. His men were scattered and not organized, and he was delving into areas he wasn't sure he'd be hailed for.

"And just a reminder," Kyle continued, "we're not even talking about all this cargo coming off here, but, if you like, we can start an inspection process. I have enough guys to do it."

Kyle's jaw was set. The ship captain had been clearly moved and was ignoring the harbormaster. He shook hands with Captain Higby again, and they saluted one another. Higby again saluted Kyle and headed for the helicopter where Dr. Solvang and his family had already loaded. The others were loaded onto the other two choppers.

Everyone watched in silence as they took off and headed northeast toward the waiting destroyer. Trace was relieved that, so far, there had been no violence, but that didn't mean somebody wouldn't be coming for them later on.

Carefully, the team receded from the dock, leaving the harbormaster and the captain to themselves. The Civil Guard took no action and allowed them to just walk through their line of defense, over to their vans. Noticing Guerrero's Jeep was missing, Kyle and the rest of the group loaded in the two vans and took off for the home base.

Once inside his vehicle, he turned around and addressed the team. "I am hoping Guerrero is arranging something for us, some kind of protection, which I didn't ask him for. But he's gone, and I don't think he wants to be publicly involved any longer. I'm okay with that. I just want to get the hell out of this country. I'm going to wait for orders when we get back, and—if everything's okay—we're going to boogie out of here and head over to the airport."

"What did you tell the captain and the harbormaster?" asked Fredo.

"I told him we had received word that criminals had been involved in the hijacking and killing of villagers in Nigeria and that the Afrika Korps was asking for the names of people complicit. I promised them that if they allowed the safe passage of the prisoners their names would not be turned into the international forces. Whether or not they would actually do something is sort of a moot issue at this point, but, when you involve the United Nations and other countries and somebody else looking over your shoulder, all of a sudden a local dispute becomes something that can be quashed from a distance. They made the right move. I don't know how long, but—for right now—they were spared. But we got the members."

Kyle received word that no further action was required and they should pack up and head for the airport immediately where a transport plane had been given permission to land. Kyle told the group after his phone call, "Well, it won't be a comfortable ride, but at least it'll get you home."

Trace wanted to call Gretchen to let her know the good news, but he decided to wait until he was on the plane to do so. He hoped that everything at home was completely settled. He couldn't wait to get there.

CHAPTER 16

G RETCHEN SPENT THE rest of the early morning accompanied by a team of police, forensics experts, the coroner, Gus Mayfield, and several of his friends from the force.

She sat on the couch in the living room and answered questions *ad nauseam*. Angie stayed by her side, but Gretchen wanted her there mostly because she knew that the police would separate her from her mother and ask her other questions. Not that they had anything to hide. She just wanted everything to get uncomplicated real quick. She was heading to collapse. She needed a shower. She needed to get some rest. But she needed Trace most of all.

Gus Mayfield was true to his word. He and several of his former colleagues arrived at the house even before the 911 crew arrived. They stayed away from the body of the intruder but counseled her on how to handle the onslaught of police and personnel who were about to descend upon her.

But she was still inconsolable. She felt like the ground had been pulled out from under her. Now possibly even Tony's life was in danger, although Gus told her otherwise.

"It's all over the station, Gretchen. Nobody's going to touch Tony. He's been put in an individual holding cell, and, unless somebody has some kind of access that I don't know about, he should be untouched until he can get properly arraigned and released. I don't know all the story of what's going on, but you certainly had justification to shoot this man in your house, and this is his gun, not yours. You do have a right to defend yourself, under certain circumstances, and this meets those criteria. It's pretty evident he came to do damage."

"If they know where I live, then there'll be others looking as well. Does this mean I have to move or go into hiding somewhere?"

"I don't have an answer for that, sweetheart. I'd like to say no, but I don't know. I'm not sure where this guy was in the pecking order of things. But the detective took his wallet and identification. We've run some checks, and this guy, Sam, has a long rap sheet. I don't think you're going to have any trouble yourself, but I can't speak to some of these jerks who Tony's got himself involved with."

"Where is Sven? Has anybody called him?"

"I think you should be the one. Why don't you do it now before more police arrive?"

So Gretchen called, but it went to voicemail. Then she called Kelly's cell phone—reaching her—and gave the updates. Sven was on a plane, headed to San Diego, she was told.

"Gretchen, I'm so sorry about this. He'll be able to tell you what further steps you're going to need to take. When does Trace get back?" asked Kelly.

"I have no idea. I can't get ahold of him either. You know, when he's on these ops, sometimes I don't talk to him for days. Just, of all the time for this to happen, of course it'd have to happen when he's gone."

"Well, as in all ops, the unexpected is what is expected. And Tony made all this happen. He is really a loose cannon. Something has to be done about it. Maybe for his own good, he should go back to jail."

"Well, he's certainly afraid of that."

"As he should be."

Around eight in the morning, after some of the personnel had started to recede, Gretchen was greeted with the face of Sven Tolar, who rushed to her side and gave her a hug.

"I am so sorry you had to go through this. I had no idea Sam knew where you were. How do you think this happened?"

"One of the detectives said a neighbor's security camera caught Tony hanging around the outside of the house. He must have parked around the block and walked up. They found shoe prints like he was wandering around, a different size from the Sam guy's. Maybe he was trying to talk to me? But he changed his mind. I guess somebody followed him here, so that's how they found out where I lived. It was Tony again."

"Of course it was. And then he went off to go get drunk and find a hooker. What an asshole. What a liability to society."

Gretchen looked down at Angie, who was sleeping on the couch fitfully.

"I just was trying to protect her, even from all these things being said about her father. I don't know how she's going to take all of this, but it's more than I can handle right now. I just want to make sure that we're safe and that we can sleep."

"You can. If they're done with you, you go upstairs and shower and go to bed. I'll be downstairs. I've got some calls to make, some things to arrange, and I will see you when you get up. Don't worry about anything."

"Is it just you? I mean, what if they send a whole army over here after me? Will they have a whole gang that shows up at the house? Am I supposed to worry about that now?"

"I doubt it, but I have the cops on speed dial. Gus

here has his crew who will stand watch until I get my people in place, at least temporarily."

Gretchen did feel somewhat relieved.

"You remember, we have the sale of the house and they're gonna get their money back. The problem now is who do we give the money to? And if we give the money to this person over here, what is this person over there going to say? Is he going to demand more money? Do you see what I mean? So I have to determine who gets paid off and why and where."

"I understand. So you'll have to go back to Portland or Eugene, is that correct?"

"I'm thinking they will reach me somehow. I mean, they do have my numbers, so we'll see. And if their connections are as good as they say, they're going to know Tony's in jail and he's untouchable. Not that it would make any difference."

"Well, they do need Tony to sign the papers to sell the house. If they kill him, how does that happen? And that ties the money up even further."

"I didn't think of that, Gretchen. Well, that may be Tony's protection for right now. And maybe we can impose on the police the bigger picture—the issue of your safety and the sale of the house and that he's needed elsewhere. Maybe we can get him an escort or they'll release him to me. I don't know. But we'll work out something. You just go take a shower and go to bed. Let me take your cell phone in case Trace calls, because I'd like to speak to him, and I don't want him to wake you up."

Gretchen handed Sven her phone, lifted Angie up, and helped her go upstairs to the bedroom. She laid her on the bed and went in to take a shower.

It felt good to have the warm water sluice down her body. She was so tired and so anxious from all of this. What she needed was a vacation away from all this crap, all this pressure and the worry. Trace was in harm's way and so was she, without him here. And that was the worst part, she thought. She could handle him being in places that he was trained to be in, with the team trained to protect him, but here at home? There was nothing set up and no one here truly to protect her. The police were so easily compromised she wasn't sure who to trust, and she really wanted to trust them. Trust somebody. She trusted Sven, but then he wasn't law enforcement. He had no official capacity.

She dried off and looked at herself in the mirror. "God, you've aged ten years, Gretchen. He's going to come home to a wild hag who mumbles and drools." She watched herself crying in the mirror.

When will this stop? she thought.

She climbed into bed and sunk into the nice, warm, lavender-scented sheets and pillow. This had been her sanctuary. This had been the place she had hoped to welcome Trace back to, help bring him back to San Diego life, to their life and their hopes and dreams and plans for the future. This had been a happy bed, a place of memorable worshiping of each other's bodies. Now she was reduced to soaking up the energy of past experiences here, begging for help, asking for God's protection, and begging also for that little kernel, that little flame of encouragement that would let her know that all would be well.

That someday, somehow they would be done with all of this.

CHAPTER 17

T RACE LANDED IN Norfolk, exhausted and sore, with a splitting headache he traced to not drinking enough water.

He checked his phone and discovered a message from Gretchen.

"Oh, Trace, things have really unraveled here. And I hope by the time you get this message that it's all cleared up, but Tony called me, and he's in trouble again. Apparently, he came down to San Diego and then got arrested. He's worried about them catching him in jail and doing something to him. I don't know what's going on. But I'm getting really exhausted and tired of all this. I just wish you were here to help counsel me. He asked me to put up money for his bail since he thought he'd be killed in jail, and I refused. I hope I did the right thing. It's actually the only thing I could do without you being here. So when you are someplace where you can talk to me, please give me a call."

Now that he was on the ground, he placed that call to Gretchen immediately. It was late morning on the East Coast, which meant even earlier on the West Coast, about 9:00 a.m.

"Hey, Trace, I'm glad to hear your voice," said Sven.

"Sven? Why are you answering Gretchen's phone?"

"Because she's upstairs trying to get some shuteye. We had quite a bit of activity last night. Apparently, Tony came down to San Diego and hung around here, got himself into trouble again, got arrested, and he's at the San Diego Central North Jail. And please hold onto your seat a bit and wait until I'm finished with the whole thing, because you're going to react. Sam showed up at the house."

"At Gretchen's house?"

"Yes, at your house, Gretchen's house, where you live with Gretchen and Angie."

"What the fuck! What's happened, Sven, and how did all this come undone? I thought you had a handle on this?"

"I understand how you feel, Trace, and I would feel the same way, but hear me out, please, before you go reacting. First of all, I didn't know Tony came down to San Diego. He was supposed to lay low and hang on to his money and wait for the house to close, and then I was going to accompany him, and we were going to deliver the cash. It would all be over. All he had to do was wait a few days, maybe a week. Everything was on track."

"That son of a bitch!"

"Hold on there, Trace. There's more. A lot more. All the conditions of the escrow were met, and we were just waiting for the funds to come through to close it. However, Tony being Tony, I guess he got a little homesick or something. He came down to San Diego. I really think he was going to try to get reconnected with Gretchen, but he never got that far. He got drunk, and he kind of wasn't thinking, and he hooked up with a San Diego decoy for prostitution, got himself in jail. And then of course getting bailed out was a problem for him because he can't remember where the rest of the money is. And he didn't want to call me, so he called Gretchen."

"Goddamnit, Sven. You didn't hear it from me, but I think the first thing I need to do is get rid of that son of a bitch. I mean permanently, don't you think?"

"You didn't mean that, Trace. That's not the right way. You know that. So here's what's happened. When Sam showed up at the house, your well-trained wife, and thank God for that, shot him with his own gun."

"Shot him? I mean, is he dead?"

"Oh, quite dead, yes."

"In front of Angie?"

"Yes, unfortunately. She was up the stairs, but she heard it all. Angie's tough, and I think she'll be traumatized for a bit, but she knew her mother was protecting them. The guy was a jerk apparently, according to what Gretchen told me, and I think the police have got the right angle on it. Gus Mayfield was called in, and I think he's helping to grease some skids here. The problem I'm having, Trace, is I got to find out who gets the money now that Sam's out of the picture. And that is a big problem, because if we give it to the wrong person and someone else shows up with his hand out, we've got a shit storm going on. Plus, we'll be out of money, and we didn't make any headway. So that's what I've got to try to figure out. And I'm in the middle of making some calls and trying to see what I can do. You're going to need some help around the house, some guards to protect her and Angie and possibly the other two girls too. I'm sorry to say it, but it's true, Trace. You can't do it all."

"Yeah, but I can't afford all this protection, Sven."

"Consider it a loan against our friendship. Trace, I really want you to think twice about what you're doing on the Teams, and I love you to death for being a warrior and a patriot for your country, but I think you could do a lot more if you were out of the Teams. If you could handle some of the scourge that now is coming into this country. You know, we used to be the place where nothing happened. But ever since 9/11, all of a sudden the barriers are cracked open, and we got all these idiots running around doing stuff, causing chaos. And the response to all of that is going to be a more heavy-handed government intrusion into everybody's lives. It's to all of our benefit if we can help quell this chaos and this mood of destruction. It's really sad and painful to watch, being a citizen of another country."

"I've thought a lot about it, Sven. I think I'm nearly there. I think Tyler is as well."

"Well, you just get yourself back to San Diego, and don't worry about anything else for right now. I took her phone so she could get some rest, and she really needs it. I know she wants to see you, so the best thing you can do is get here and get with her. That's the only thing that will console her. And Angie needs you too. I'm arranging the protection for Rebecca and Clover, and I've already talked to her husband about it, and he's all for the protection. I haven't been able to get hold of Rebecca yet, but I'm close. So just get home, Trace, and try not to worry."

"Fat chance of that, with all this news. Sven, I wish I'd never left."

"Hence what I was saying, Trace. You belong on our team here. You don't belong clear across the world.

You're no longer a Boy Scout. You're a protector, you're someone who needs to protect his own, and we live in an increasingly hostile and volatile environment here at home, unlike ever has happened before. Never did I ever expect to see your country dissolve into this chaos. And local authorities are way outmatched, outgunned, outfought, outfinanced. It's just not a conclusion that's going to have a happy ending. You got to be here to protect what you love. You got me?"

"Loud and clear, Sven."

It took several hours before Trace could arrange his transport back, but he finally took a commercial flight nonstop to San Diego. He checked in with Kyle before he left.

"I'm sorry, Kyle. We got chaos at home, and this thing with Tony is just blown way out of control. I don't know how long I'm going to be involved in it, but I'm sorry I won't be available much for debriefing, but I'll do what I can."

After Trace told Kyle all of the particulars, especially Gretchen's sure shot on Sam, Kyle was most understanding.

"Well, you get it sorted out, and then we'll talk. I knew this was going to happen someday, Trace. Nothing is forever, is it?"

Trace felt tears form in his eyes. It made him mad, but he continued on anyway. "Nothing is forever, but we do our best to try to prolong death. That's sometimes, I think, the only thing I know how to do in life."

"Now give yourself some credit, Trace. You're far more than a killing machine or a death-defying machine. You're a lover, and you're a husband. A good husband and a father to girls who deserve and need you. Without you doing what you're doing, they'd be left in a puddle of shit. And you're helping to clear that up. There's no way the Navy or anything I could offer would entice you enough to pull your focus off of that. That's your prime directive. I don't blame you one bit. But don't sign any papers or do anything stupid as far as telling someone you're going to quit. You talk to me first, and then we'll work out some kind of an agenda, and maybe there's still a place for you somehow. But first things first, you take care of your wife and kids, and you see if you can help Sven get this fire put out."

"Thanks, Kyle. You know I learned how to deal with all of this under your guidance. If I hadn't seen some of the crap we've been through on these missions, if I hadn't seen how you held up with all these bad guys, how you ran our team, how you respected us, I would never have the cojones to do what I'm doing now. You trained me for this."

Kyle sighed. "Yeah, I'm sorry about that. I guess I wish I didn't do such a good job. But you go do yours. And we'll talk. I'll be praying for you."

When Trace landed in San Diego, he gave a call to Sven to let him know he was on his way. He picked up his Hummer and drove straight home after texting Kyle to let him know that he was back.

He parked in the driveway behind two remaining police vehicles. He didn't care that he blocked their access. Running to the front door, he dashed into the living room and found Sven sitting at their dining room table making calls and notes on a lined pad Gretchen had given him.

"Where is she?"

"They're upstairs questioning her. She's okay, Trace. Let them do their job," said Sven, standing to come over and greet Trace properly.

"Fuck that. I want to see her."

Trace dashed past Sven up the steps, taking two or three at a time, and crashed through the closed door to their bedroom.

"Trace!" Gretchen screamed as she ran to him. They collided in the middle of the room. She was shaking, sobbing with tears. Angie timidly stood by the side and Trace included her in their embrace. He got down on his knees. "Thank God my girls are okay. Did anybody hurt you, Gretchen? Are you okay, Angie?"

"No. Now that you're back, we're fine. Scary. It's going to take a while, Trace. But we're just trying to figure out what to do now. Do you think we have to leave?"

"No fucking way. This is our house. This is where

we make our stand."

Trace heard someone clear their throat behind him, and he stood up and turned to face two uniformed San Diego police.

"I'm supposed to take pictures of the girls, make sure they're not injured."

Trace looked at Gretchen, who nodded her agreement.

"Get it over with," he sighed.

One by one, each of the women went with the female officers to the rest room to have their nude bodies photographed. Angie was allowed to wear her underwear.

"Thanks for your cooperation, ladies. Now, Trace, I'm going to give you my card. They'll have to come downtown and answer questions, make statements."

"They're not under suspicion, are they?"

"Not supposed to comment, but no, sir. Not as far as I can see, but you didn't hear it from me, understood?"

"Thank you. We'll cooperate."

"You might also want to get a good attorney, just in case. I doubt it will be needed. Again thanks for your patience, and thanks for your service, Mr. Bennett. I wish we had more like you here on the force."

"That's not my gig."

"Well, you take good care of each other, and we'll be in touch." The two officers left.

When they were alone, Gretchen whispered, "I don't think they're after me, Trace. I'm worried about this Organization. Has Sven found out anything yet?"

"I don't know. I ran past him, and I suppose he's got something for me, but that's not nearly as important as seeing you guys. I am so grateful that you're okay. I am never going to leave you guys alone like this again. Never. We're going to stay all together. And we're going to fight this thing. I don't care what it takes."

"Does that mean the Teams?"

Trace cut her off. "No decisions. Everyone knows I'm thinking about it. No decisions yet. Let's get this job done, and then we go on to the next one. Okay?"

"Absolutely, sweetheart."

"How much rest have you had?"

"I don't think I could go back to bed. Maybe I'll turn in early tonight, but there's just too much going on. Every little sound, every little thing that goes on, even a distant siren, I'm up. I'm alert. I can't function, Trace. I think the only thing I can do is just let time take care of me. And now that you're here, it'll be much better. Dear, go downstairs with Sven and let me get dressed. Angie and I will come down and join you. Maybe we'll make some lunch or something."

"You don't have to do anything, Gretchen. We can make something. Don't worry about it."

He noted that Gretchen's cheeks did begin to flush a bit now that he was in the room, and he hoped that Angie's glum expression turned around. But he was going to give them time, plenty of time to heal and get used to the new reality of their lives.

Because of what Tony had done, everything had changed. Now, instead of being an old fuddy grandfather enjoying his first grandchild, he was going to have to be looking over his shoulders all the time. And for this he knew he was going to need help. He decided to face the music and ask Sven what the score was. He halfway didn't want to know it, but it had to be done.

Sven hung up the phone and looked up.

"So, Sven, what do you have for me?"

"So far it's good, Trace. I got hold of someone who's agreed to take the funds, and I think I trust him, but we'll know further before it is time to release them. My guys did some inquiring up in Eugene, and turns out, this guy, Sam, was really the right-hand man of another fellow, an Albanian fellow who was always in the shadows. I think he's going to be easier to work with than Sam was."

"Well, that is progress then. When's the meet?"

"Well, first, we have to get Tony out of jail so he can sign the papers. My understanding is that they are just waiting for him. Escrow is ready to close."

"Thank God."

CHAPTER 18

G RETCHEN WAS GOING to give Angie some time to herself. She found her listening to music while she read one of her favorite books.

"What would you like to do today, sweetie?"

"I just want to have a normal family. I want to feel safe. I don't want to worry so much."

Gretchen sat on the edge of the bed, noting her pale complexion and dark bags under her eyes. Angie's room was done in pale pinks and greens, with posters, letters, pictures from friends, and lots of family pictures, especially ones with her sisters in them, hanging on the walls. It was a happy room, but the child living inside it was not. Gretchen reached for her hand.

"I am going to work very hard to make sure you have this, Angie. It's been a lot for all of us. Now that Trace is back, I hope some of the stability we felt before will come back. He is so much a part of that for us now, more than before. And with Tony—"

"I don't ever want to see him again, Mom. He's a complete loser. I'm embarrassed to have him as a father. Don't make me, okay?"

"I won't."

Gretchen felt the same way, but he was her children's father, and, in the event Angie changed her mind someday or Tony had a miraculous transformation, which wasn't likely, she would have to keep the connection quietly open. She knew it was going to be Angie's decision and wasn't hers to make. But she'd honor her request for now.

"I was thinking we could go down to the beach today? Gather shells? Trace needs a beach day too."

"Sure, whatever. Or we could just stay here. Are Clover and Rebecca coming over soon?"

"Would you like that?"

"Yes."

"Okay, let me see what I can do." She watched Angie put her earbuds in and open her book again. Leaning forward, she kissed her on the forehead. "I'm making some food downstairs. Should I bring you something?"

"I'm good," she said loudly, due to the music in her ears.

She patted her daughter's thigh and closed the door behind her. Worry traveled down the stairs with her. Entering her master kitchen, she began to make some fresh coffee.

Sven and Trace were still sitting at the table.

"Anyone want coffee?" she asked.

"Let me make it," Trace said as he started to get up.

"No, you talk. I'll join you when I get the coffee made. Both of you?"

"Not for me. I would love a beer if you have one, Gretchen," said Sven.

"Coming right up. I'm going to put out some fruit and cheeses. Anyone want some eggs or a sandwich?"

"Nah, just beer for me. Too late for breakfast," Sven scowled.

Trace shrugged. "Whatever you bring I will gratefully partake of, sweetie," he said at last and sat back down.

She put together a platter of fruit with some mangos and papayas she'd bought at the farmers market, added some grapes and unsalted crackers, with sliced cheeses made with peppercorns and herbs. She set it on the table with napkins in front of the two men, who began devouring it, just as she had expected they would.

The teapot squealed.

Bringing in the two steaming mugs, each filled with tons of cream, she sat beside Trace at the table. "What's the plan, Stan?" she asked.

"Sven was just telling me about the meeting he was

setting up. How's everything upstairs?"

"Angie is still a bit quiet. She's reading, listening to music. She did ask if we were going to have the girls come over. Do you think we should make it a family day? Sven, should we have a talk with them about what the new normal is going to be? Or what it would be for now?"

Gretchen knew he wouldn't like being put on the spot, but she was advocating for her girls.

"Not a bad idea. We don't have to worry about forgetting something when we instruct the girls. There are going to be changes, you know that. At least temporarily."

Gretchen leaned in. "Please explain all this to me. I've been in a fog."

"Understood." Sven swung his computer around so Gretchen could see the faces of several men. "These are members of the Berisha crime family, an Albanian group which has been here for many years. They have family units located all over the U.S. and Canada, as well as Europe. They are a criminal enterprise. They partner with various other groups, some political, some just crime-related. They pick and choose to whom they partner, depending on their needs.

"In this case, they own a business that brings in girls from the Middle East and Africa, through their contacts there. They partner with another group in

Seattle for gaming and sports betting and work with various casino groups, including some Native American tribes. It's a conglomerate. They can move easily around the globe, have amassed enormous assets and clout, pay off local officials, and try to eliminate people who stand in their way. Let me repeat what I've said earlier. They are extremely dangerous."

"So it's not about the politics or the power. It's about the Benjamins," said Trace.

"Exactly. They don't want to be in power, play that game. And if one of their partners starts to cross the line, they will either walk away or eliminate the competition. But they've learned how to work with other groups, not against them, and that makes them very effective."

"How the hell are we supposed to fight them?" asked Trace. "Seems impossible to me."

"In a word, carefully. Getting themselves in the paper or having their wings clipped is not good for business. We can't take them out, but we can be a bee in their underpants and cause them some pain."

"And they'd back away?" Gretchen asked.

"Theoretically," Sven said with a long face. "I wish I could tell you that it will be easy or quick. But, unfortunately, this is not the case."

Gretchen felt the ache in her eyes as her tears started to swell and then spill over onto her cheeks. Trace put his arm around her. She was glad he hadn't tried to sugarcoat it or said something about not worrying about it. It was her primary concern. Her family had gotten into the clutches of a dangerous flesh-eating entity. And she'd just killed one of their henchmen.

"So what does that mean for me? For Tony?"

"I don't have all that yet. They mainly want the money. That's the goal. The rest is collateral, complication to them."

"So we have to become their complication," said Trace.

"Yes, partially. I think we have a hidden ace. You, as a Navy SEAL and with the SEAL community behind you, you could cause some disruption to their little program. And some public attention since the public, at least for now, is with you guys. You are the good guys. We use that, leverage it to the highest so that they find it in their best interests to behave."

"How do we do that?" Gretchen wanted to know.

"There's a story there to be told. A good story. One of their members came after the wife of a Navy SEAL and her fourteen-year-old daughter. Huge public sentiment against this kind of thing. After all, you did nothing to harm them; it was your stupid ex. They perhaps don't have a code of ethics, but I doubt they'd want the public scrutiny."

"So we go public with it. Have Gretchen interviewed," said Trace.

"Exactly. Your police colleagues don't want that, I'm sure. But I doubt they have the resources nor the manpower to do a thorough investigation either. It's a hot potato for them. Perhaps this gives them, too, a way out. No one does time for the crime, but everyone walks away whole as they can be and leaves each other alone."

"Until Tony crosses the line again," swore Trace.

"Or someone else. If we go picking off their people, the Bone Frog group now becomes a target. I'd like them to be oblivious to our existence. I doubt they know anything about us. But they do know the SEALs. And that might be enough."

Everyone was silent for a few minutes. Gretchen, oddly enough, suddenly felt somewhat hopeful for the future.

Then Sven's cell rang.

"Tony, nice to hear from you. Is it all arranged?"

Sven put the phone on speaker and placed it next to their fruit platter.

"They said someone made my bail. But I want to know, who is going to pay for that asshat coming over to my ex-wife's house and scaring the shit out of her? They've got to pay. I've been telling everyone down here that it will be my mission in life."

Sven shook his head, held his hands up to Trace

and Gretchen.

"Then it will be a very short life, Tony. If you have the burden of the money debt off your shoulders, can you live a straight and narrow life? Can you behave?"

"Behave? How about how they've behaved? That can't go unpunished. That has to be atoned for first, Goddamnit!"

Trace covered his face with his hands.

"So are you ready to be picked up?" Sven asked.

"In a few minutes. I'm filing charges against that asshole."

"But he's dead, Tony. Sam's dead."

"I'm gonna sue the bar and grill. Sam's assets. I'm gonna take it all, man. I'll get my money back if it's the last thing I do!"

"Tony, I'll come get you, and we'll have to talk. Don't do anything until I get there. Let me get you back to Portland, so we can complete the money transfer. I understand you have papers to sign."

"Sweet! I'll be rolling in dough then!"

"Tony, you do understand that money's committed now. It was supposed to go toward your children's education, Tony. It's not really your dough to roll in. It belongs to your girls, in reality. So don't get too cocky about it. Don't gamble away their lives as well as your own."

"That's a valid point. I'll certainly take it under

consideration. So when are you coming down here?"

"I'll be down there within the hour. Don't sign or fill out anything, and I mean anything. I'll bring an attorney with me just to make sure everything is as it should be. But sounds like they got the bail money. Let me ask you this. If we can get the charges dropped, will you stop this ridiculous notion of going after the bar and grill?"

"I'll consider it."

"It might be your only option."

"No, sir. I met a lot of guys in here who know these guys, and they even said they'd help me get even!"

"Right after they report you to get a lesser sentence. You're way over your head, Tony. The sooner you figure that out, the less dangerous it will be for the family."

"By the way, can you arrange a meeting with Gretchen and the girls? I'd like to see them and apologize."

"Not my call. I'll see you soon. And remember, try to keep your mouth shut and don't sign anything. Agreed?"

After a pause, Tony hesitated and agreed.

"You see how it goes?" Sven said. "He's not capable of doing anything wise. Just not in his nature. He's so flawed I don't think anything could save him."

"You're right. And he's getting worse," added

Gretchen. How could she ever have fallen for him in the first place?

"Problem is, it shades on everyone else in the family. We have to do something about that," said Trace.

"And that's what we're going to do. It might take a little time, but I think there is a path. We just have to put all the pieces together. I doubt they do the kind of in-depth research we do. But, on the surface, if they look into you and the SEALs and how Gretchen is so tightly woven in that community, I'd think they'd stop there and end their vendetta against you all."

"Until Tony kicks the hornet's nest again," sighed Trace.

Gretchen was still hopeful but cautious. "He's like a drunk driver who gets into accidents. Everyone else gets killed, and he survives, somehow. The further down he spirals, the more dangerous he gets too. Wish someone would just get rid of him."

"You never said that, hon," whispered Trace.

"I didn't hear it either," answered Sven. "No talk like that, Gretchen."

She was thinking to herself that she got rid of one bad guy and discovered within herself she wasn't remorseful. Maybe she could get rid of another. Someone had to stop Tony or he would destroy them all.

She had to protect her girls.

CHAPTER 19

TRACE'S EMOTIONS WERE cresting all over him, adding confusion to his reunion with Gretchen and the girls. She'd invited everyone to come over, and, after Sven left, they began playing Monopoly, Angie at last coming to life as she began fleecing everyone with her ruthless play and lucky rolls of the dice.

There were accusations of cheating, arguments about the rules, and passing Go mishaps with the bank, which was Gretchen, leading to more accusations of cheating and fraud. In the end, it was all good fun. Even Jack got in the groove, playing his own game piece and, at times, conflicting with his new bride.

Clover was blushing more, happier than Trace had ever seen her now that she was carrying the new little one. He was struck with how precious his family was now, how it was growing, stemming from his love of this wonderful angel who had come into his life and saved him in every way possible. How was it that his love for them could fuel his desire to kill? But that was happening. He wanted to protect the precious loved ones he was gloriously compelled to safeguard.

Jack was watching him. Sometimes it made him nervous. But he'd never raised a son, and he took advantage of feeling that wonderful connection passed down through the ages: how a man brings a boy into manhood, makes him more of a man so he could train his own boys. The true circle of life. Perfect as perfect could be.

And still there was much to be worked out. Sven and his crew would be working overtime in the coming days so that, when the transfer came, all the counter plays would be covered, just like in a game of chess. Certain pieces would be protected, others sacrificed. Making the final decisive move was important and strategic.

And Tony was always going to be the wild card that could flush all their plans, the devil who changed all the plays at the first engagement, just like in battle. Wishing it wasn't so was a waste of time. Best to face it straight on and prepare, overprepare even.

He'd seen Gretchen come into this psyche as the hours went by, saw the warrior woman strength she'd always had but never trained. She was strong, perhaps even stronger than he was. It was awesome to see.

Kyle had once told him that he thought Christy was stronger than he was, that he'd known it the first time he met her. Trace could say the same.

"It's the hardest job you'll ever have, having a strong woman like that. Well, that and having children. Both are hard, but you'll love it even more."

Kyle was right. All good things were work. They were a practice. There was no cause, no mission that could be completed as planned—it was always a dance, looking for the opportunities and making the most of it. The worst thing to do was to become unconscious or to stop feeling.

And that's how Trace could justify being a killing machine. It was worth it. He wasn't dead inside. He was alive and honorable. He would always maintain that SEAL ethos. He was just that ordinary man who did extraordinary things. He did things others couldn't do, not because he was better, just because he could.

If there was a way he could stay as a SEAL and still work with Sven and his team, he wished he could. That would have to come later but soon. Kyle deserved to have an answer, and Sven was investing so much into his future, he felt he owed him as well. It was a hard, yet dangerous, problem to have.

At least he had a choice. And, whatever choice he made, it would be perfect.

He got a text that Sven and Tony were safely on their way to Portland. He would call with updates tomorrow. Sven was exhausted, but he needed to get Tony up to his compound to keep an eye on him.

Trace commented with a thumbs-up and a praying

hands emoji. "Thanks, brother," he texted and signed off.

Gretchen's phone rang. She got up to take the call in the kitchen. When her turn came up on the game board, everyone started calling to her.

"Just a minute, please," she answered from the kitchen. Trace could hear something in her voice.

He checked in on her. Her back was to him, and she was wiping tears from her eyes.

"What's up, Gretchen. Are you okay?"

She turned around, and he could see the tears, along with a happy, crazy smile. "What an amazing few days we've had, huh?"

"Yes. It's normal. You're on overload." He took her into his arms, even though the room called to her again. "Just a minute," he shouted back, with Gretchen clutched to his chest.

She sobbed, then stopped. He felt her spine stiffen as he released her to examine her face again.

"That was the doctor's office calling. Remember, they asked me to go get checked out for the police report?"

"Yes, something wrong?"

"No, not really." She placed her palms at the sides of his face. "Trace, sweetheart, I'm carrying your baby. We're going to have a baby, Trace."

Did you enjoy Second Time Love? I hope you will continue on with the story of Trace and Gretchen as they work on their new challenges while solving the problems of the past—still very much in love and with that love growing every day. Stay tuned for a Christmas novella coming out toward the end of the year, "Christmas Miracle."

It will be posted here when it comes out.

authorsharonhamilton.com/seal-brotherhood-legacy

You'll have answers to some of your questions and a continuation of new issues and problems that arise as this family copes with their collective hopes and dreams. You'll see Trace continue to protect his loved ones and the other innocents of the world he's tasked with saving as Gretchen becomes the warrior partner he's always needed in his life.

Lots of twists and turns ahead, so stay tuned!

ABOUT THE AUTHOR

NYT and USA Today Bestselling Author Sharon Hamilton's SEAL Brotherhood series have earned her author rankings of #1 in Romantic Suspense, Military Romance, and Contemporary Romance. Her other *Brotherhood* stand-alone series are: Bad Boys of SEAL Team 3, Band of Bachelors, True Blue SEALs, Nashville SEALs, Bone Frog Brotherhood, Sunset SEALs, Bone Frog Bachelor Series, and SEAL Brotherhood Legacy Series. She is a contributing author to the very popular Shadow SEALs multi-author series.

Her SEALs and former SEALs have invested in two wineries, a lavender farm and a brewery in Sonoma County, which have become part of the new stories. They also have expanded to include veteran-benefit projects on the Florida Gulf Coast, as well as projects in Africa and the Maldives. One of the SEAL wives has even launched her own women's fiction series. But old characters, as well as children of these SEAL heroes, keep returning to all the newer books.

Sharon also writes sexy paranormals in two series: Golden Vampires of Tuscany and The Guardians under the pen name S. Hamil. She has a new Sci-Fi series, Free to Love, which came out in June of 2023 in a five-book ultra-spicy series about an android who falls in love with a human woman.

Annie Carr, Sharon's sweet romance author pen name, released her first book early in 2023: I'll Always Love You, in Sunset Beach stories. She is planning this to become a multiple-book series.

A lifelong organic vegetable and flower gardener, Sharon and her husband lived for fifty years in the Wine Country of Northern California, where many of her stories take place. Recently, they have moved to the beautiful Gulf Coast of Florida, with stories of shipwrecks, the white sugar-sand beaches of Sunset, Treasure Island, and Indian Rocks Beaches.

She loves hearing from fans through her website:
authorsharonhamilton.com

Find out more about Sharon, her upcoming releases, appearances and news when you sign up for Sharon's newsletter.

Facebook:
facebook.com/SharonHamiltonAuthor

Twitter:
twitter.com/sharonlhamilton

Pinterest:
pinterest.com/AuthorSharonH

Amazon:
amazon.com/Sharon-Hamilton/e/B004FQQMAC

Life *is one fool thing after another.*
Love *is two fool things after each other.*

REVIEWS

PRAISE FOR THE
GOLDEN VAMPIRES OF TUSCANY SERIES

"Well to say the least I was thoroughly surprised. I have read many Vampire books, from Ann Rice to Kym Grosso and a few other Authors, so yes I do like Vampires, not the super scary ones from the old days, but the new ones are far more interesting, far more human than one can remember. I found Honeymoon Bite a totally engrossing book, I was not able to put it down, page after page I found delight, love, understanding, well that is until the bad bad Vamp started being really bad. But seeing someone love another person so much that they would do anything to protect them, well that had me going, then well there was more and for a while I thought it was the end of a beautiful love story that spanned not only time but, spanned Italy and California. Won't divulge how it ended, but I did shed a few tears after screaming but Sharon Hamilton did not let me down, she took me on amazing trip that I loved, look forward to reading another Vampire book of hers."

"An excellent paranormal romance that was exciting, romantic, entertaining and very satisfying to read. It had me anticipating what would happen next many times over, so much so I could not put it down and even finished it up in a day. The vampires in this book were different from your average vampire, but I enjoy different variations and changes to the same old stuff. It made for a more unpredictable read and more adventurous to explore! Vampire lovers, any paranormal readers and even those who love the romance genre will enjoy Honeymoon Bite."

"This is the first non-Seal book of this author's I have read and I loved it. There is a cast-like hierarchy in this vampire community with humans at the very bottom and Golden vampires at the top. Lionel is a dark vampire who are servants of the Goldens. Phoebe is a Golden who has not decided if she will remain human or accept the turning to become a vampire. Either way she and Lionel can never be together since it is forbidden.

I enjoyed this story and I am looking forward to the next installment."

"A hauntingly romantic read. Old love lost and new love found. Family, heart, intrigue and vampires. Grabbed my attention and couldn't put down. Would definitely recommend."

PRAISE FOR THE
SEAL BROTHERHOOD SERIES

"Fans of Navy SEAL romance, I found a new author to feed your addiction. Finely written and loaded delicious with moments, Sharon Hamilton's storytelling satisfies like a thick bar of chocolate." —Marliss Melton, bestselling author of the *Team Twelve* Navy SEALs series

"Sharon Hamilton does an EXCELLENT job of fitting all the characters into a brotherhood of SEALS that may not be real but sure makes you feel that you have entered the circle and security of their world. The stories intertwine with each book before…and each book after and THAT is what makes Sharon Hamilton's SEAL Brotherhood Series so very interesting. You won't want to put down ANY of her books and they will keep you reading into the night when you should be sleeping. Start with this book…and you will not want to stop until you've read the whole series and then…you will be waiting for Sharon to write the next one." (5 Star Review)

"Kyle and Christy explode all over the pages in this first book, *[Accidental SEAL]*, in a whole new series of SEALs. If the twist and turns don't get your heart jumping, then maybe the suspense will. This is a must read for those that are looking for love and adventure v ʰ a little sloppy love thrown in for good measure."
Review)

PRAISE FOR THE
TRUE BLUE SEALS SERIES

"Keep the tissues box nearby as you read *True Blue SEALs: Zak* by Sharon Hamilton. I imagine more than I wish to that the circumstances surrounding Zak and Amy are all too real for returning military personnel and their families. Ms. Hamilton has put us right in the middle of struggles and successes that these two high school sweethearts endure. I have read several of Sharon Hamilton's military romances but will say this is the most emotionally intense of the ones that I have read. This is a well-written, realistic story with authentic characters that will have you rooting for them and proud of those who serve to keep us safe. This is an author who writes amazing stories that you love and cry with the characters. Fans of Jessica Scott and Marliss Melton will want to add Sharon Hamilton to their list of realistic military romance writers." (5 Star Review)

"Dear FATHER IN HEAVEN,

If I may respectfully say so sometimes you are a strange God. Though you love all mankind,

It seems you have special predilections too.

You seem to love those men who can stand up alone who face impossible odds, who challenge every bully and every tyrant ~

Those men who know the heat and loneliness of Calvary. Possibly you cherish men of this stamp because you recognize the mark of your only son in them.

Since this unique group of men known as the SEALs know Calvary and suffering, teach them now the mystery of the resurrection ~ that they are indestructible, that they will live forever because of their deep faith in you.

And when they do come to heaven, may I respectfully warn you, Dear Father, they also know how to celebrate. So please be ready for them when they insert under your pearly gates.

Bless them, their devoted Families and their Country on this glorious occasion.

We ask this through the merits of your Son, Christ Jesus the Lord, Amen."

By Reverend E.J. McMalhon S.J. LCDR, CHC, USN
Awards Ceremony SEAL Team One
1975 At NAB, Coronado